Mushoku Tensei

redundant reincarnation

1

WRITTEN BY
Rifujin na Magonote

ILLUSTRATED BY
Shirotaka

Isolde
Dohga
Linia
Pursena
Ghislaine
Rudeus
Lucie

Ruijerd
Norn
Sylphiette
DRAMATIS PERSONAE

"The name of
the Doldia tribe
has helped
me and never
hindered me.
I bear no grudge."

Mushoku Tensei
redundant reincarnation

WRITTEN BY

Rifujin na Magonote

ILLUSTRATED BY

Shirotaka

Seven Seas Entertainment

MUSHOKU TENSEI ~DASOKUHEN~ Vol.1

Illustrations by Shirotaka
First published in Japan in 2023 by
KADOKAWA CORPORATION, Tokyo.
English translation rights arranged with
KADOKAWA CORPORATION, Tokyo.

Seven Seas press and purchase enquiries can be sent to Marketing Manager Lauren Hill at press@gomanga.com. Information regarding the distribution and purchase of digital editions is available from Digital Manager CK Russell at digital@gomanga.com.

Follow Seven Seas Entertainment online at sevenseasentertainment.com.

TRANSLATION: Saba Kan
ADAPTATION: Lorin Christie
COVER DESIGN: Nicky Lim
INTERIOR LAYOUT & DESIGN: Clay Gardner
COPY EDITOR: Meg van Huygen
PROOFREADER: Jack Hamm
EDITOR: Laurel Ashgrove
PREPRESS TECHNICIAN: Melanie Ujimori, Jules Valera
MANAGING EDITOR: Alyssa Scavetta
EDITOR-IN-CHIEF: Julie Davis
PUBLISHER: Lianne Sentar
VICE PRESIDENT: Adam Arnold
PRESIDENT: Jason DeAngelis

ISBN: 979-8-89160-510-7
Printed in Canada
First Printing: November 2024
10 9 8 7 6 5 4 3 2 1

CONTENTS

NORN'S WEDDING

CHAPTER 1:	Norn's Betrothal (Part 1)	11
CHAPTER 2:	Norn's Betrothal (Part 2)	37
CHAPTER 3:	Norn's Betrothal (Part 3)	57

LUCIE AND DADA

CHAPTER 1:	Lucie's First Day of School (Part 1)	81
CHAPTER 2:	Lucie's First Day of School (Part 2)	101
CHAPTER 3:	Lucie's Family	123

THE SEVEN KNIGHTS OF ASURA

CHAPTER 1:	Isolde Looks for a Husband	133
CHAPTER 2:	Dohga the Gatekeeper	155
CHAPTER 3:	Isolde and Dohga	179

THE WOMAN THEY CALLED THE MAD DOG

	The Woman They Called the Mad Dog	205

"Even if one's life looks easy from the outside, it can be tumultuous for the one living it."

—It may seem like a calm life, but it's tough.

AUTHOR: RUDEUS GREYRAT

TRANSLATION: JEAN RF MAGOTT

Norn's Wedding

CHAPTER 1
Norn's Betrothal (Part 1)

A FEW MONTHS HAD PASSED since the battle in the Biheiril Kingdom. The Man-God kept quiet after what happened, and as time passed, no new enemies made themselves known. That didn't change my job, of course. I quietly kept up my travels, laying the groundwork for the war with Laplace eighty years from now.

Even so, I'd been at home a lot lately because, as it turns out, Eris and Roxy were both pregnant at the same time. I kinda cut loose after defeating Geese, so I guess you reap what you sow! While I was happy with the way things turned out, it had been said that pregnancy would weaken their destinies and made them easier targets for the Man-God. So while my wives were pregnant, I wanted to be by their sides as much as possible.

In the meantime, I spent my days processing the intelligence that came in from the mercenary band outposts around the world, meeting with Orsted to discuss our next moves, and enjoying some long-overdue family time.

This is a story from one of those days. Orsted and I were having a meeting about what we knew regarding my next destination. It was something about how the next in line for the throne of that kingdom was still young, yet showed promise. It seemed like a good idea to start putting things in motion now, so we could put him to good use later.

Orsted stayed silent without offering any comment on how to win over the next ruler. I figured he must have had his reasons. Maybe there was some person key to pulling it off who wasn't in this loop. Or it could be that he thought there was no surefire way to do it right now, so we should wait until a later point in time.

So what should I do?

I looked down at the notes I'd taken based on the portrait that Orsted had painted of this amazing heir and thought hard.

Just then, he spoke.

"Have Norn Greyrat get married."

"Wha...?"

Out of nowhere, Orsted broke his silence with this bizarre statement.

Although I was being careful with how I spoke around Orsted, I still almost blurted out, "What the hell are you talking about?!" It was that jarring.

Right now, we were thinking about how to win over the amazing heir. What Orsted said was totally irrelevant. But then I started to wonder... Was it really irrelevant?

And then it occurred to me.

"Do you mean," I said slowly, "a political marriage?"

It was the only thing that made sense with the conversation we were having.

"I wouldn't call it political, but when I consider the future... Well."

"So you're saying...I can't do it alone?"

That was frustrating to hear. It meant Orsted had decided I couldn't talk this amazing heir into an alliance. I wouldn't have minded if he said that outright—hell, even I wasn't confident I could do it by myself. I had no idea what I could even say to sway him. If he were a skirt-chaser like Paul, and the only way to get him on our side were to give him a woman, then Orsted's proposal would have made sense.

But Norn was out of the question.

I knew Norn would get married someday, but there was no way I would hand her over to someone who was a womanizer like Paul. Norn had to marry someone more... earnest. And I had to approve of him—no way I'd just ship her off to some random guy. I'd never be able to face Paul again. You never cast aside family for the sake of a goal, no matter how lofty.

"No," Orsted said.

"Then why?"

"The child of Norn Greyrat was a help to me."

"Help...? So this has nothing to do with Norn; you need her child?"

"I do not need it. The child will not be of great importance in this loop."

He was dancing around the point. Orsted always spoke in riddles, but based on our other conversations up until now, I got the gist of what he meant. Basically, this was groundwork. Norn's child might not be important, but it had been useful to him in past loops, so he would make the play just in case—something like that.

"Very well." I stood up. I looked down at Orsted, who was still seated and looking up at me. He wasn't wearing his helmet. He had the same scary look as ever, but I bet my face was even scarier.

"If you are going to insist on this, then come to the northern forest at noon three days from now."

Fear not, Norn. I shall defend your virtue. I will stand my ground, even if I have to face Orsted. Paul, please... Give me strength. Give me the strength to vanquish this mighty foe and live to tell the tale.

"Wait. You misunderstand."

"I do?"

"Even I, in the course of these endlessly repeating two centuries, have people for whom I care. Norn Greyrat's child is one such person. She has helped me, coming to my aid time and time again. It is for this reason that I wish to grant her life in this world. As things are, this will not come to pass."

It was true that I never saw Norn with boys. She'd graduated, but she was still living at home, same as always. That wasn't to say she was freeloading, however. Through her school connections, she'd joined the magic guild and was doing clerical work at their central branch. There were plenty of guys at the guild, but Norn didn't seem to care for them. She never went out, even on her days off; rather, she was always at home helping with the kids or the housework. Even as a student, I didn't think she'd dated anyone.

I honestly thought she might go her whole life without ever tying the knot.

Hmm. In this world, people with status seemed to do arranged marriages a lot, and while mine was a bit sketchy, it *had* provided me with connections and influence. Maybe this wasn't such an outlandish proposal.

"Okay, but a child isn't made by one person. It's not like any old partner will result in the same child being born, right?"

We were talking about a king, so he had plenty of status, but I wasn't going to consent. Not until I'd seen him with my own eyes and checked out what sort of man he was.

"Or does this amazing heir become Norn's partner in the future?" I asked, glaring at Orsted. He was frowning. His expression was as scary as ever, but I'd seen this look before. It was his "What the hell are you talking about?" face.

The ends of his eyebrows twitched as though in surprise, and he said, "No... Forgive me. It is unrelated to that."

"Huh?"

"This is another matter."

Another matter...? Ah, that's what he meant?

"So this wasn't about our strategy for the next country? We're just talking about Norn's love life?"

"Yes."

Huh. Well, all right, then.

"Sir Orsted."

"Yes?"

"When you change the subject, it's good to lead into it with something like 'Changing the subject,' or 'By the way...'"

"That is true. I will be careful in the future."

With all that smoothed over, I settled back into my seat.

I collected myself, then got back to the conversation.

"So who is it that Norn marries? Does she always marry the same person?"

"Yes. As far as I am aware, Norn Greyrat's husband never changes."

So Norn and this person were destined to be together. Lucky bastard. Just living his life, and then all of a sudden, he gets to marry my Norn. If he turned out to be a lazy bum coasting through life, I'd kidnap him and straighten him out—Spartan-style. I'd make sure he did nothing but train from the moment he woke up in the morning until he fell asleep. By the time I was finished with him, he wouldn't be able to say anything but "yes," "please," and "thank you." No way he'd cheat on her then.

At minimum, anyone who wanted to marry Norn would have to take a punch from Eris without passing o—

"Ruijerd Superdia."

My thoughts screeched to a halt. I saw in my mind's eye the face of a bald man who'd lived around five hundred years.

Scratch that—he wasn't bald anymore.

A handsome man with a handsome head of green hair.

"Their child becomes the last Superd warrior. After Ruijerd succumbs to plague in his later years, she carries on his quest to restore the honor of the Superd, joining the human side to fight the demons. She is the one who deals the finishing blow to Laplace. Her fate is heavy, painful, and goes unsung by all... But in this loop, many of the Superd have survived. In all likelihood, no great burden will fall on her shoulders."

While my mind sat frozen, Orsted's words poured out as he remembered the girl's life. If she defeated Laplace, she and Orsted had probably worked together. And if so... Yeah, I could see why Orsted had brought this up.

But okay, now what? It was different this time around. I was here, and the displacement incident had happened.

However Norn and Ruijerd's relationship had developed in previous loops, if I knew one thing, it was that in this loop, it hadn't blossomed into the love story Orsted knew. If I suggested marriage to Norn out of nowhere, she might just balk. I mean, it was a five-hundred-year age gap. It would probably confuse Ruijerd too.

I wasn't going to complain about Ruijerd joining the family, but I couldn't just go making a decision like this myself. No, definitely not.

"If you ask me," I said slowly, "I think Norn gets the final say."

"Very well. There is no rush," Orsted answered with a nod.

After that, he told me about Norn in all the loops up until now. In the worlds where I didn't exist, Norn became an adventurer. On her adventures, she performed songs and wrote ballads as a bard who could sing, dance, and fight. She and others with similar interests formed a party and traveled around the Northern Continent. Her sword and magic skills were marginal at best. B-rank was her limit. Because of that, while they were in the middle of some quest, her party was wiped out by monsters.

Norn herself was inches from death when who should appear but our very own Ruijerd. He tore through the advancing monsters and saved Norn's life. For Norn, it was love at first sight. After that, she joined him on his journey to find the Superd.

At first, Ruijerd hadn't been responsive, but then he discovered that the Superd had all been wiped out by a plague and fell into despair. Norn devoted herself selflessly to comforting him, which in turn won her Ruijerd's heart, and they got married. They began their life together in a corner of the Biheiril Kingdom. After a while, they had a child, then Ruijerd contracted the same disease as the other Superd and died, leaving Norn behind. She raised their child, then died of old age.

It sounded like a lonely, bittersweet life, but Orsted said there had been a look of contentment on her face. As a love story, it was hard to swallow, but what goes on between a man and a woman is something only they know.

Things hadn't gone that way for Norn this time. Was it still okay to set her up with Ruijerd? Would Norn be happy with someone she didn't love? Would Ruijerd be open to it?

There was no point in me worrying about it on my own. The important thing was how Norn felt. She didn't show any sign of interest in boys, but she was the right age for romance. One day, she'd suddenly bring him home, and the little punk would say, "I've come to ask Norn's father for her hand in marriage." Then I'd say, "Who're you calling 'father'?" Or "I'm her *brother.*"

But I'm getting off topic here.

I had the feeling I wasn't the right person to ask Norn about this sort of thing. I couldn't see her opening up to me. Another woman would be better—just not Aisha. I had the feeling that if I sent her, it wouldn't end well. Sylphie or Roxy, then? Norn respected Roxy in particular, so maybe Roxy was best.

Eris might work too, if we were talking about respect. She'd been teaching Norn swordwork for a long time. Every morning since she graduated, Norn had been out with Eris jogging and practice sparring and what have you. You only had to look at them together to see how Norn admired Eris. Unfortunately, I doubted Eris's move list included the "indirect question" skill.

No, it had to be Roxy. *Wait, hold on.* The one with the high "indirect question" stat was Sylphie. And while it wasn't quite respect, Norn did seem to recognize Sylphie as the top dog in this house.

Or maybe I should just consult all three of them... Yes, the four of us could work together to decide who was best suited to the task. It'd be better to get Sylphie, Roxy, and Eris's opinions. But were the three of them enough? Should I talk to Lilia and Zenith too?

I mulled it over on the living room sofa.

"Oh." My eyes fell on a woman who'd come into the living room—Norn.

"I'm back, Big Brother," she said.

"Welcome home." She'd grown up beautiful. She looked just like Zenith had when she was younger, with sizable breasts and silky blonde hair. I bet she'd been popular with the boys at school.

"What...?" Norn asked after a while.

"Nothing... Um, Norn, want a cup of tea?"

"Yes, please."

I picked up one of the cups on the table, quickly filled it with tea, and then handed it to her. As Norn accepted it, a dubious look came over her face.

"This is cold."

"What?!"

Didn't I just have Lilia make me a pot? I touched the teapot, and she was right. The cup in my hand was cold too. *What's going on here? Is someone attacking me?!*

"Wait." A thought hit me. "Come to think of it, didn't you have work today?"

"Yes, I just got home now."

I looked out the window. It was already dusk. My meeting with Orsted had ended, then I'd come back here and had Lilia make me a pot of tea. That had been early afternoon, so two hours must have passed.

"Right, sorry. I must've zoned out."

"I'd appreciate it if you waited until you're older before going senile..." Norn teased. "I'll make another pot. Wait there, Big Brother."

"Is no one else home?"

I was sure Sylphie and Eris had just been here. And Roxy... Okay, at this time of day, Roxy wouldn't be home yet.

"Sylphie and Eris left just as I came back to take the children for a walk. Lilia went shopping."

"Aisha?"

"I don't know. She's probably still with the mercenary band, isn't she?" Norn said as she carried the teapot off to the kitchen.

Right, okay. No one's home. Just me and Norn... In a way, I couldn't have asked for a better situation. Yeah, I'd tackle this head-on. No beating around the bush. If that didn't work, then I'd move on to the next thing. That was how I would be honest with Norn.

Right. Yeah. Norn wouldn't like it if I only talked to her after I'd set everything up. I mean, *she* was the one getting married.

I had to start with Norn.

"Here you are." While I was lost in thought, Norn came back, setting a cup of tea down in front of me.

"Thanks." I watched as she sat down directly opposite me, then took a sip. "You've gotten good at brewing tea, huh?"

"We learned how to at school."

"Not from Lilia?"

"Lilia… I don't think she would teach me."

Well, yeah. If she asked Lilia to teach her how to brew tea, she'd probably say there was no need because that was *her* job.

"I'm sure she would if you asked."

"Perhaps. But seeing as the school had a place to learn, I took advantage of it. Besides, I never have the chance to make tea at home."

"I guess so."

She'd had student council meetings and her room at the dormitory, and now probably her workplace too. She seemed content with that.

Anyway, now that I'd warmed things up with some light chitchat, I wanted a good way to broach the main topic. What to say? Where did I begin?

"Umm... Ahem, uh-hrmm..." As I cleared my throat, Norn looked at me dubiously.

"Was there something I neglected?" she asked.

"N-no, not at all. Very nice tea." I took another gulp from the steaming cup. The flavor wasn't anything amazing, but it wasn't bad enough to make me want to spit it out. It was ordinary, just like Norn. Good, but not great.

In other words, nice. But leaving that aside...

"By the way, Norn, how...how've things been lately, hm?"

"What things?"

"Well, your job, for example. How's that?"

"Everything's normal. A senior staff member is still teaching me the ropes...but I think I'm doing well enough. Of course, I'm sure Aisha would be doing far better."

"You ought to stop comparing yourself to her," I said. Norn nodded obediently. Aisha had her own work. So long as they weren't doing the same job, comparisons didn't do anyone any good.

"Now, this senior staff member..." I went on. "That's a thing, eh? Cool, I bet?"

"Oh, very elegant. I think the two of you spoke once, Big Brother. Yes, you remember the deputy student council president from when I was president?"

"The... The burly beastfolk kid?"

"Not him. The woman."

Oh. A woman. Right. The name wasn't coming to me, but there *had* been someone like that. Actually, I had the feeling Norn had brought it up when she got the job. Something about how they were in the same department.

"A woman, eh... Don't happen to be any men around, hmm?"

"Of course there are."

"And are any of them...you know...cool?"

"Some are, some aren't."

So there *was* someone cool. This was big.

"Big Brother, what are you getting at?"

"Calm down, there, Norn. No need to rush to conclusions."

"*You're* the one who doesn't look calm," she countered.

Of course I'm calm! I'm always cool, calm, and collected. CCC Rudeus, that's me. And none of those stand for crazy!

"Norn, uh... Just for example, um, this cool person... How cool do you think he is?"

"Are you asking if I like him?"

"Do you?"

Crap. I asked her straight out.

"No, I can't say I do."

Oh, screw it.

"So is there by any chance someone you *do* like?"

There was a long pause, then—

"Yes."

There is! She told me there is *someone!*

"Y-you don't say! There is, is there? Well, you are a grown woman. Of course there is. Nothing strange there. No, sir."

"You, on the other hand, are being very strange."

"What?"

I'm not strange. It's everyone else! This world is strange, not me!

"So what's he like, hmm?" I went on. "This person you like?"

"He's...older."

"Uh-huh."

"I can depend on him."

"Uh-*huh*..."

"And he always takes care of me."

Take those three criteria, and you get...

"Do you mean me?"

"Is something wrong with your head?"

Sorry. Got carried away.

"He's *much* older than you, Big Brother, and he never loses his cool in a crisis. He's composed and dignified."

"You know, lately, your Big Brother has also stopped losing his cool in a crisis."

"I don't think you get to say that considering how you've been acting."

Oof...

But okay, she said much older than me and dignified? Damn...

"By much older...you mean, what, ten years older than me?"

"Older."

"I...didn't know you had a daddy complex."

"A daddy...? Well, I *do* like older men."

By "older," I guessed she meant more than twenty years older. That would put him in his forties or fifties. Add "dignified" to that, and I was thinking of someone on the heavier side. With a lower center of mass, you get a real sense of gravitas. Not that I was anywhere close to "dignified" in my past life.

I was picturing something like an old man with a greasy face who was CEO of an evil trading company.

I wasn't about to criticize anyone over an age gap, but no matter how I looked at it, it sounded like she was looking for a sugar daddy.

I won't stand for it, hell no!

But hold on. What if this guy turned out to be more sincere than I thought...? An age gap was nothing, really. You can't judge people by their looks.

"But I've accepted that nothing will come of my love."

"Oh... Is he married or something?"

"No... He said he lost his wife..."

Lost, huh? Maybe that was a convenient way of saying he divorced her. Or maybe *she'd* just slapped *him* with the divorce papers.

...I was working hard to avoid accepting the truth.

"Apparently, I remind him of her."

Okay, in that case, it can't be. Yeah, no way. He wouldn't say something like that.

"That's one of the oldest lines in the book."

A man catching a much younger woman and telling her she looked like his dead wife? What else could it be? He was basically saying she was the sort of girl he could see himself marrying.

Hold on, though. It didn't really sound like a pickup line when you thought about it. Something about how she was nothing like his wife, how he'd never met a girl like her before... That'd be a better line.

"...Are you asking if I've been seduced?" Norn put her hands to her cheeks, which were a little flushed. Was she happy about the idea? Oh, right. Norn liked him, not the other way around.

But Norn, he might be leading you on. There'd be a fight if I said anything right now, so I kept the thought to myself.

"Why all these questions all of a sudden, anyway?"

"Huh? Well, that's..."

"You're up to something, aren't you?" Norn glared at me. It was a look that said she'd been honest, so now it was my turn. I hadn't expected her to be so open. I'd have been happy to just gather she liked someone from her reaction.

"Well, I don't want to bring it up right after what you just said..."

"Okay." As I leaned slightly closer, Norn drew back in turn.

"The truth is, Norn," I said. "I've had a sort of marriage proposal for you."

For a few seconds, Norn froze. Her eyes were wide, and her lips pursed in a frown. It was like she was glaring at me.

"A proposal..." she repeated. "Very well. I accept."

"No, I get it. Say no more. After what you said? Let's pretend I never brought it up."

"No, like I said, I accept."

I stared at Norn, the doubt probably clear on my face. "But you...you already have someone you like, don't you?"

"That doesn't matter. After all, it's never going anywhere." Norn seemed to consider for a moment, then continued. "We aren't nobility, but you have status, and my friends told me something like this might come along one day. Besides, ever since I found out that you have connections all over the world, I've expected to be used like this."

"I didn't say 'use.' I'm not going to make my family into pawns," I said a little heatedly. Norn's eyes widened, then she bowed her head.

"Of course... I'm sorry."

Such a good girl.

"Norn, if you say you don't want this, then we ditch the idea."

"No... I'm not against it. The fact that you've come to talk to me must mean the other person isn't a bad man, right?"

"Well, I guess."

He wasn't a bad match... At least, I didn't think so. They'd seemed to get on well during the battle in the Biheiril Kingdom. Ruijerd was an honorable man.

"Only... Well, my heart isn't set on getting married, but I'm not dead against it either. I would be grateful if we could pretend this never happened, Big Brother, if you'd do that for me. Of course, if the other person insists, then you should go ahead with it. You needn't worry about me..." Norn looked away.

She didn't seem to want it very much. She would do what I said if I asked, that was all. That might be convenient for me, but not for her.

"I haven't run it past the other person yet, so it's fine."

"I see... Thank you."

Sorry, Orsted, but if it's what Norn wants, then we ditch this idea.

After a moment, Norn added, "By the way, what sort of person was it? Were they some sort of royalty? Or an Asuran noble?"

"No, nothing like that... But you know him, Norn."

"I do...? Oh, do you mean Zanoba?"

"I don't think he's the marrying type."

Zanoba was best left alone. Even with Julie blasting him with her love beam, he showed zero signs of interest in her, much less Ginger. He probably planned on spending his life with his figurines.

"It was Ruijerd," I said, revealing his name.

Before I knew what was happening, Norn was leaning toward me, both hands on the table. There was an intense look on her face, which flushed bright red. She looked angry.

What was that about? Had I said something to offend her?

Norn did seem to have a lot of respect for Ruijerd, so it seemed she didn't think of him in that way after all.

Right. Sorry, Norn. Your big brother messed up. You can stop glaring at me like that now.

"Hey, look, it was silly. Even setting aside that he's a different species, the age gap is too big, and even you—"

"Please accept the proposal!"

Norn cut me off, her voice brimming with excitement and delight.

As it turned out—or sure enough, I should say—the object of Norn's affections was Ruijerd.

Apparently, she'd adored him since she was little, and that childhood crush had developed into romantic feelings. And while in the Biheiril Kingdom, she had reaffirmed her feelings: she was in love with him.

But Norn, knowing Ruijerd's past, had assumed he wouldn't reciprocate. She'd resigned herself to spending the rest of her life hiding her true feelings.

I put a hand to my chest and said, "Got it. Just leave it to me."

Mushoku Tensei
redundant reincarnation

CHAPTER 2

Norn's Betrothal (Part 2)

LEAVE IT TO ME.

With those words, I went straight to laying the groundwork for the marriage. Norn was on board, so now the only question mark was Ruijerd. Considering his age, he ought to leap at the chance to marry my little sister. Plus, marrying into my family would serve the Superd too. Since days of yore, marriage had often served to solidify alliances. A marriage between Norn and Ruijerd ensured the Superd wouldn't turn against the Dragon God, and on our side, it meant we wouldn't abandon the Superd. It was a win-win situation.

But still, was that enough? And would this make Norn happy? If Ruijerd married her because he had to, would that be what she wanted? Could she hold back her tears when she realized he didn't love her?

Currently, Ruijerd was responsible for the negotiations with the Biheiril Kingdom. That meant Norn would live not in the Magic City of Sharia, but in the Superd village. At least after what happened there, all the villagers seemed to know her face and name; they would probably welcome her. But would Norn be able to cope surrounded by people of a different species and an entirely different culture from Sharia? Worst case, Norn might even end up living alone in a nearby town.

I was worried. Genuinely worried.

When I asked my wives about it, Roxy said, "It's Norn. I'm sure she'll be fine," Eris said, "It's Ruijerd. They'll be fine," and Sylphie said, "You're overthinking it."

They were sure it would be fine, but still, I worried. I couldn't bear Norn being unhappy. If she ended up crying, I'd have to face Paul's resentful gaze in my dreams while Zenith sat at my bedside and slapped me in my sleep. For their sake as well, I had to give Norn the best chance to be happy—but even then, it would be up to her what she did with it.

I could trust Ruijerd, of course. I knew that even if he didn't truly love Norn, he would give her everything she was due as his wife. He would ensure she had no reason to cry. Still, I needed to be sure. What if I set up an event to nudge the two of them together? I might be able to steer Ruijerd's feelings toward Norn and make sure they would be happy.

"Right," I said to myself.

That was how I ended up in the Biheiril Kingdom in the Superd village. Just a few months earlier, it had been under heavy construction, but now it was back to looking like a village again. It was surrounded by a tall palisade, within which there were houses and empty vegetable patches. When the Superd warriors saw me, they bowed their heads and warmly welcomed me into the village. I nodded back at them by way of greeting, then hurried off to Ruijerd's house. It was a new build, of course.

Ruijerd's house was big, maybe because he was a fairly important person in the village now. Yep, this was plenty of space for two—and kids.

"Ruijerd," I asked tentatively, "are you home?"

"Rudeus?" he answered. Maybe he'd just finished a meal—he was sitting cross-legged in front of the hearth, his eyes shut as though he'd been meditating.

Without a word, I sat down in front of him. I was kneeling. At that, Ruijerd opened his eyes and looked at me questioningly.

"What is it?" he asked.

I held up a hand to him. "Give me a moment, please. I'm working out what to say."

"All right."

I lapsed into silence, staring into the flickering flames for what felt like an hour. Strange as it sounds, I hadn't given any thought to what I should say. I knew what I had to ask: How did he feel about Norn? Did he like her? Hate her? Could he see himself marrying her?

The question was how to say it. *Wanna marry Norn?* Something like that? No, scratch that. Getting married and how he felt were two different issues. I couldn't forget that.

I stayed quiet, but Ruijerd didn't try to make conversation. He patiently waited for me to speak as though we had all the time in the world. I didn't know what he had to do that day, but he was a busy man. He'd be like this with Norn too, I was sure. Maybe Norn would get annoyed at him for it. Maybe she'd snap at him to say *something*.

Nah, it was probably that side of Ruijerd that Norn had fallen in love with. A person you can be comfortably silent with is a rare thing. Though, admittedly, I was a bit uncomfortable.

"Norn made me tea the other day, and she was actually quite good at it," I said, fishing for a reaction.

"Well, well. Norn making tea."

A nibble from Ruijerd. Maybe he was interested in Norn after all. Had I cleared the first hurdle, then…?

Hold on, though. If a guy says something after being silent for a full hour, of course you'd latch on, no matter what he said.

Settle down, Rudeus. Conversation is all in the flow.

"Apparently, she's always making tea at work, and that's how she improved."

"I see… I once drank tea she made when she came to the village. It *was* very good."

Ruijerd smiled at the memory. So he'd had Norn's tea before, had he? Maybe he wanted to drink it again. Maybe he was thinking he'd like her to make it every day just for him…

Dammit, how do I ask the question? I could do with some options. Is this how Orsted feels when he talks to me? How the heck do I do this?!

"Not only can she make tea, her cooking isn't bad either."

While I hesitated, the conversation still flowed.

Wait just a minute. What was that? Home cooking?

"You've tried her cooking?"

"I have."

Norn's *home cooking? When even I've never tasted it?*

"You don't say..."

I wondered what she'd cooked. Meat and potato stew? Curry? Maybe beef stroganoff? I wanted some too. I wanted to taste Norn's home cooking!

Never mind, this wasn't about me.

He said it "wasn't bad," which meant it hadn't been a disaster. Maybe she wouldn't find her way to his heart through his stomach, but it seemed she wasn't a total failure in the kitchen. I wouldn't see Ruijerd waste away after the wedding, then.

"Has something happened with Norn?" Ruijerd asked, cutting through my thoughts. How perceptive of him.

Well, okay. After I'd come in here looking all serious and brought up Norn out of nowhere, I guess it was the obvious question.

"No, um... Nothing in particular. I was just, you know, making small talk."

Unfortunately, I didn't quite have the courage to ask him straight-up yet.

Do you like Norn? Do you love *her? Could you take her in your arms right this second and kiss her?*

What if I asked, and he said he didn't like her at all? That he couldn't marry her, and even if he did, he wouldn't love her...? I couldn't help but wonder. It'd be a major shock for me, for sure. I might start a fight right here. *You saying my Norn isn't good enough for you?!*

"Norn's an adult now and even has a job, but in some ways, she's still very much a kid... I mean, she doesn't seem to have any interest in guys at all. I sometimes worry if she'll be able to find a husband, you know?" I said, then looked at Ruijerd. Maybe I'd been too obvious—Ruijerd looked suspicious.

Eventually, he said, "Is it not human custom for the choice of marriage partner to be left to the head of the family? Are you not the one who will choose Norn's husband?"

"No, no, no. We aren't nobility, you see. I kind of feel like it might be good to let Norn choose a husband for herself, kind of, um..." I stole a glance at Ruijerd, but his expression hadn't changed. Actually, no. There was a hardness on top of the suspicion now. He didn't think I was shirking my responsibility, did he?

"No, don't worry! If Norn brought back some good-for-nothing, I'd throw him out on his ear. I'd tell him, 'If you want Norn, you'll have to go through me first!' I'm not about to hand Norn over to just anybody!"

I rushed to make an excuse. It'd be a disaster if Ruijerd thought I was irresponsible just before I offered him Norn.

I couldn't think exactly how it'd go wrong, but it absolutely could.

"You mean to say that anyone who wishes to take Norn for a bride must defeat you first?"

"No...! He doesn't absolutely need to be strong or anything! But! It's just, well, how should I put it... Grit! That's it, I want him to show me he's got grit."

Heck, I was a coward, but I didn't run. Anyone who wanted to marry Norn had to have the guts to stand and fight even when he knew he couldn't win. That was it.

"Is that so?"

"It is."

Obviously, Ruijerd had nothing to worry about there. I tried to convey that to him with another surreptitious glance, but his face was immobile—the hard look hadn't wavered...

Maybe he wasn't interested in Norn after all. It was probably only natural. To him, Norn was a child. Ever since they'd met when she was little, she'd always been a weak child. And Ruijerd wouldn't lust after a child. He wasn't that sort of guy.

"Ruijerd, I... I'm just going to ask straight-up."

"Very well."

I mean, I still had to ask. Just in case. Even if it ended up being too bad for Norn. I couldn't jump to conclusions based only on his expression. Time for me to bite the bullet.

"How do you feel about Norn?" I asked.

Ruijerd was silent. He glared at me, not saying a word, his expression hard as stone. The suspicion was totally gone.

Hmm. That was weird. Usually, I'd have expected Ruijerd to answer straight away. Did he consider her a child or an adult?

I steeled myself.

"Do you...have feelings for Norn?" I had to be blunt. Had I made a mistake? Maybe it would have been better coming from Norn.

"Ah," Ruijerd murmured. Then, as though making up his mind, he got to his feet. He took his spear from where it stood propped up.

"Rudeus," he said at last. "Go out the front."

I looked up at him, not comprehending what he meant.

In response to my hesitation, Ruijerd said in an even stronger tone, "Go out."

"All right." The intensity in his voice left no room for argument. I readily obeyed.

We left the Superd village and walked for fifteen minutes or so into the forest of the Ravine of the Earthwyrm.

Deep in among the trees, the forest suddenly opened on a clearing. There, Ruijerd and I faced one another.

Ruijerd's expression had been grim the whole time. Maybe I'd made him angry somehow. It seemed that asking him if he had feelings for Norn after that talk had been a mistake after all. I guess he thought I was offering Norn up for the sake of politics or something. This was Ruijerd. He'd be a man and say, "As her older brother, Norn is yours to protect. Do not use her to curry favor with some stranger." He was reliable like that.

"You realized long ago, then."

This was unexpected. I stared at him blankly. What had I supposedly realized? What was I supposed to have realized? Me, the guy who right now, at this very moment, was totally lost and confused? Me, who you couldn't call perceptive even to be nice?

"Realized what?"

"There is no need to say more. Prepare yourself!"

When people said, "no time to protest," this is what they meant. I obviously didn't have the Eye of Foresight open, and without it, there was no way I could keep up with Ruijerd.

"Yow!" Ruijerd was on me in an instant, sending me sprawling on the ground. Still, compared to a decade or so earlier, I was a better class of loser. My daily training regimen paid off—I was just barely able to react. Ruijerd's spear had come slashing from the right. I blocked it with the Magic Armor Version Two's gauntlet. Ruijerd followed up with a low kick that I raised one leg to block, leaving me standing on one foot. He twirled his spear around to take out my pivot leg with its butt.

"Well?" Ruijerd pressed the point of his spear into my neck, looking down impassively at me.

"I give up. You win."

I had no idea what he was asking. There was nothing else I could say. I was pretty sure he wouldn't stab me through the throat, but I'd lost.

"Was that good enough?"

What are you talking about? Was what *good enough?*

"If anything, I think it was me who wasn't good enough."

"It...was sufficient, then?"

What was supposed to be sufficient? He'd knocked me down like it was nothing. I'd only embarrass myself if I tried to say any more.

"I think so," I said. With that, Ruijerd drew his spear back. I pushed myself up to a sitting position. Even I could tell how pathetic I must have seemed as I looked up at Ruijerd.

Then, he said something bizarre.

"Then as promised, I claim your sister."

Claim? My sister's hand? What about my sister? Did I promise that? Hold on. What are we talking about again?

The thread of the conversation had slipped away from me a bit.

"It is as you suspected."

What did I suspect?

"I would be bound in wedlock with Norn."

"Wed...lock..." I desperately tried to remember what that meant. Right. Matrimony. The state of marriage.

"Huh?" So Ruijerd loved Norn?

Hold up. Don't get ahead of yourself! You've got a bad habit of getting things mixed up.

"You mean, you...about Norn..."

After a long pause, Ruijerd said, "I love her."

Was it possible he was joking? Was he planning that I'd be so delighted, I'd tell him I agreed to him marrying Norn on the spot, and then when I actually brought Norn in dressed in her bridal kimono, Ruijerd would pop up, saying "You got punked!"? It'd be a crushing emotional blow for me. Norn might even take to her bed. This was the Man-God's plot, for sure.

Damn it all, Ruijerd was a disciple of the Man-God!

"Are you joking? Or is this some sort of prank?"

"This is no joke," Ruijerd said, looking a little offended. He never joked, and this was no exception.

"Since when?" I asked.

"Since the battle in the Biheiril Kingdom several months ago. She selflessly tended to me at that time."

It was true—they'd been inseparable back then. Very domestic. But had that really been more than a one-sided attachment on Norn's part? I thought maybe she'd hung around mooning over him while he was oblivious.

"I did not act on my feelings, of course."

Would he have acted if she hadn't been my little sister? I guess so. That was what happened in the usual loops, according to Orsted—and then Norn would become a woman, a bride, and a mother.

"But you realized, I see. I assume that is why you came here so abruptly and asked."

I was silent.

He's gotta be kidding. All I knew was that Norn loved him—I had no idea it was mutual. I have the perceptive powers of a brick.

"I reiterate: it is my wish to take Norn as my wife." Ruijerd raised the spear he'd held to my neck. "To that end, I have demonstrated my grit."

Oh, so that's what this was? A duel, to show me his grit?

But it was like...how do I put this? It was too easy. Everything was going too smoothly. *Is it a trap? Who's trying to trap whom? I have no idea. What's going on here?*

I spoke sitting right there on the ground while looking up at Ruijerd. "...Is it all right with your last wife and your son?" Because I didn't understand, I decided to keep asking questions.

"I am not clinging to the past."

It did ring a bell that he'd told me he just hadn't met the right person.

When I didn't stand up, Ruijerd stabbed his spear into the ground, then sat down cross-legged beside me. I shifted to kneeling. Now our eyes were on the same level.

"In other words..." Ruijerd said just that, then he frowned and looked down, pressing his lips together.

After I'd shown up out of nowhere and exposed his true feelings, he'd made up his mind to go on the offensive and brought me all the way out here to show me his mettle. However, he'd never been good with words. He was probably still working out what he wanted to say, what he ought to say.

Maybe I'd rushed this. I hadn't needed to set the two of them up straight away just because of what Orsted had told me. Maybe I should have thought up a more indirect strategy to bring them together. Like, if Norn were kidnapped, and I asked Ruijerd to save her... No, scratch that. That would only capture Norn's heart, so maybe I'd lure Ruijerd into a trap. Norn would hate me for it, though.

As I was stewing, Ruijerd spoke. "I had expected to one day marry a human."

"What do you mean?"

"Because of you, the Superd are recovering. The people of the Biheiril Kingdom and the ogre tribe have welcomed us warmly. As it was with the ogres, one day, one of the Superd will form a bond of blood with one of the royal family or the nobility. It has been proposed that in that case, the first should be me."

"Huh." They'd talked that over...? Well, that made sense. Ruijerd's position in the village was as a sort of advisor to the village head. He was an old, respected war hero. Like the village idol... Well, not quite like that, but he was sort of like a guardian angel. He would marry some Biheiril princess or noblewoman. For the Biheiril Kingdom, that'd mean peace of mind, as the Superd would then protect the kingdom.

"But if I were allowed to choose... Rudeus, I would join your family."

I felt something warm blossom in my heart. The friendship of the Biheiril Kingdom would help the Superd. No doubt it would help them far more than blood ties with my family. But Ruijerd chose my family. He chose me!

Wait, not me! Thank goodness. I was about to turn into Girldeus.

At that moment, something occurred to me.

"You're happy with Norn, then?"

"What do you mean?" Ruijerd looked dubious.

"Norn is... How can I put this? She's, well, pretty selfish. She sometimes says insensitive things without really thinking about the consequences. If, hypothetically, you had a fight as husband and wife, she might tactlessly blurt something out about your past."

Ruijerd was silent. I hadn't expected that to come out of my mouth, and I regretted it. I was here to support Norn. I needed to talk up her good points, but she did have some shortcomings.

"I think she has the hang of all the housework, but I can't say if she'll be any good at it if it's her main occupation. She can learn, but she's not very good at applying what she learns or working things out, and she usually messes things up the first time. It's easy in Sharia, but in the Superd village, I'm sure there'll be a lot to figure out. She might be a real burden."

Look, there are other women of marriageable age in my family. Like, say, Aisha. To be honest, Aisha is more talented than Norn. She can do housework, and she can look after kids. There's nothing Norn can do that Aisha can't. I can't help but wonder if you'd really be happy with Norn.

I wanted to support Norn, but I also liked Ruijerd. I wanted them both to be happy, so I needed to be sure neither would be dissatisfied.

"But that is the result of her doing her very best, is it not?" Ruijerd countered. "I know Norn. I know her strengths and flaws." I was at a loss for words. Ruijerd continued insistently. "You do too, don't you?"

"Of course."

Norn had lots of good points. I didn't know that much about what Norn was like these days, but she had learned to care about other people. People had stopped comparing her to Aisha, so she'd stopped being unnecessarily servile. She didn't get hysterical as much, and she didn't fight with Aisha anymore. She was caring too. She didn't take the respect home with her, but her classmates and the younger students admired her. She'd had lots of friends at her fifteenth birthday party. Even now, younger students sometimes came to our house to ask Norn's advice about their studies or the student council.

Norn tried her hardest at everything. She'd never be the best, but she was competent. Plenty of things didn't come naturally for her, so maybe she didn't seem like much of a catch. And when compared to Aisha, it was night and day.

But why compare them? Norn worked hard and made steady progress. She'd keep that up for the rest of her life because that was who she was. She was a good kid—a little sister I could be proud of.

Ruijerd knew how hard she tried. He didn't need me to tell him about her strengths or weaknesses or how hard she worked. He loved it all.

"Do you promise to always protect Norn?" I asked him at last.

"Yes," Ruijerd said firmly. Of course he would. He'd protect her till death parted them.

"I expect Norn will struggle after getting married, surrounded by people from a different race and separated from her family. Will you support her?"

"Yes," Ruijerd vowed. He would for the rest of his life.

"Do you promise to keep loving her even when she gets sulky over nothing and says unkind things?"

"Yes."

I bet he'd hold her through it.

"Norn follows the Millis faith... Do you promise to stay faithful?"

"Yes."

That one was obvious. Ruijerd wouldn't be swayed by any woman's charms.

"Norn's an even bigger crybaby than me. You don't mind that?"

"I do not. I will not give either of you reason to cry."

Too late. Fat tears were streaming down my cheeks. Ruijerd spoke little, but his eyes were clear. "I do not mind. I understand all of that."

The memory of our journey across the Central Continent after the displacement incident came back to me. So long as I was with Ruijerd, I felt safe. No matter what monsters came after us, Ruijerd kept us safe.

Admittedly, he had some weaknesses when he wasn't fighting monsters, but so does everyone. It'd be fine if Norn helped him in those areas. Given who she was now, I was sure she could do it. If not, Ruijerd would have never said he wanted to marry her.

The tension left my shoulders as relief washed over me.

"Take good care of my sister," I said. Then finally, I bowed my head.

CHAPTER 3

Norn's Betrothal (Part 3)

Norn

I WAS TO MARRY Ruijerd. It all happened so fast. Big Brother asked me all sorts of questions, and I answered him honestly. Then, not even ten days later, he set up a meeting between Ruijerd and me. There and then, Ruijerd told me he loved me and proposed. I felt like I was walking on air.

The arrangements went ahead for the wedding, which would be held in ten days. Big Brother and Ruijerd were steadily getting things ready, while my only job was to make my wedding clothes with the Superd women. The outfit was very Superd-style, like what Ruijerd always wore.

The wedding was to be held according to Superd custom. I'd always sort of liked the idea of a Millis-style wedding, but I wasn't unhappy about a Superd-style wedding—it reminded me I would be Ruijerd's bride. And all the Superds were wonderful people. I couldn't have asked for more. Besides, Ruijerd would probably have been uncomfortable with me kissing him on the forehead in front of people.

No matter what came up, Big Brother told me to leave it to him. I accepted it all with gratitude. Though, I did kind of want a Millis Necklace. Maybe I'd ask for one. After all, this would probably be my last chance to ask my brother to indulge me.

These were the kinds of things I pondered while I packed up my room. It was the room I had used ever since Ruijerd brought me here with Aisha. Honestly, after all this time, my dorm felt more like home than here. However, as I packed, I realized that every item held memories. There was the figurine of Ruijerd that Zanoba had given me. I'd been so thrilled the first time I laid eyes on it that I begged him for it. It had sat in my dorm room until graduation. Gazing at the doll had become part of my daily routine. It didn't look exactly like Ruijerd, but you could tell it was him. Every time I saw it, I missed him.

Then there was my wooden practice sword. I'd used it practically every day since Eris started teaching me sword fighting. I hadn't progressed much, and I knew I had no talent for it, but I didn't mind. Swinging the sword around was fun, and it wasn't as though I wanted to be the strongest in the world. Besides, no one here in Sharia told me I should give up if it didn't come naturally. Big Brother didn't, of course, and neither did Eris, Roxy, or Sylphie... Even Zanoba and Cliff didn't comment on it, despite how gifted they were.

I now understood what a great kindness they had done me, and how important it was to persevere. If not for how hard I'd worked, I could have never become student council president.

None of the student council members while I was president had any talents either. Some of the teachers called us the first student council of dunces since the founding of the university, but Vice Principal Jenius told me, "The students are far more peaceful than when Ariel was president." Truly, there was less violence and crime at the school while I was president than there had been in Ariel's time. It was possible I was just lucky, but I wonder if it wasn't *because* none of us had any talent. The fact we were dunces probably meant we could relate to the average student's needs better, and the students were considerate of the student council in return. Maybe they thought we needed their help. The university had around ten thousand students, so all those students taking a little more care would do more good than just a dozen or so student council members trying their hardest.

I never wore my school uniform anymore. It was in the closet. I'd heard that Nanahoshi had designed it. Before then, everyone wore different clothes, but now everyone, from the scariest delinquent to the most bewitching beauty, dressed the same.

The uniform helped me make friends for sure. If we'd worn different clothes, I'd never have been able to relate to everyone on the same level. With the way that demons and beastfolk and people like that dressed sometimes, I would have never even approached them... Or maybe I'm wrong. Aisha had copied the idea and brought in uniforms for the mercenary company, so that was a good sign it was effective. I mean, *Aisha* was doing it.

Then there was Father's sword, hanging on the wall. He had used that sword for years before he married my mother. When Big Brother divided up Father's belongings after his death, the sword went to me. Aisha got the other one, but Big Brother took it back straight away, saying he was going to use it in battle. The armor was in Mother's room.

Whenever anything bad happened, I prayed to this sword. Father hadn't followed the Millis faith, and he lived a life that faithful people sneered at, but I loved him. If he were still alive, I'd probably always be scolding him. Even so, I could never dislike him. He tried; he really did. But just because you try doesn't mean things will work out—not for Big Brother, not for me, not for anyone... I think that's why I never stopped loving him...

...I prayed to my father today too.

"I'm going to get married, Father," I said. This was less a prayer than an announcement. Big Brother said that he often went to Father's grave to tell him about things that had happened, even though he was so busy... I was amazed by his faith.

"Big Brother is doing everything for me in your place, Father. Up till now, I'm sure I've been a burden on him, but despite that, he's working as hard as he can, without complaint. I can't begin to express how grateful I am to him."

I had planned on announcing my wedding but ended up talking about Big Brother instead. After our father died and our mother ended up the way she did, he stepped into Father's place. Of course, he was so busy that there were times he couldn't keep an eye on me, so I couldn't help wondering if he resented the responsibility. Now, however, I knew that wasn't the case.

There's this memory I have from back before I could even crawl properly. I was competing with Aisha, I think. I'm not sure why. Mother was at the finish line, and naturally, Aisha beat me. She made it to Mother with incredible speed. Mother picked her up and told her what a good girl she was and how well she'd done. When I saw that, I started crying. My mother was so far away. I felt like Aisha had taken her from me and I wouldn't be praised, so I cried.

When I did, Mother said, "Come on, Norn. I'm here." She waited until I reached her, then she made sure to praise me.

Big Brother was the same way. No matter how slow or stupid I was, he always waited. He was patient, and although he was sometimes flustered, he never gave up on me. It was his way of filling Mother's shoes.

The wedding preparations, too. Big Brother had taken care of everything for me. If Father were still alive, I'm sure he would have handled it all. There might have been a bit of a row if he hadn't liked Ruijerd, though.

Still, I'm sure that when the time came for me to get married he would have said, "Leave it to me." That's probably what it was like when Father and Mother got married.

Lost in my thoughts, I finished packing up my room in no time. There had never been very many things in it in the first place. Without my belongings, it looked truly empty. Lucie or one of the others would have this room next. I thought it was tidy enough, so now all that was left was to move my things to Ruijerd's house in the Superd village.

Honestly, it felt like a dream. After admiring Ruijerd forever, I was going to marry him. I was full of jitters. It was like how Sylphie said it had been for her—before you start living together with a man, you feel a mix of nerves and anticipation. Ruijerd was much, much older than me, but after we got married, I assumed we would do what Big Brother and Sylphie and the others did. I'd learned how to do it in theory, but I'd never put it into practice. Would he be gentle? Would I be able to do it right? My anticipation outweighed my nerves. I was full of excitement.

I was so glad that I'd told Big Brother to go ahead with the betrothal.

There was a knock at the door, then a voice. "Hey, Norn? Got a moment?" I'd have known that voice anywhere—it was Aisha.

"Yes, what's the matter?"

"Um... Can I talk to you?" Aisha came into my room, an uncomfortable expression on her face, and shut the door behind herself. That was unusual. It might have been the first time Aisha had behaved like this toward me.

"Why don't you sit down?" I suggested.

"Mm." Aisha took a seat on the bed. I pushed aside the luggage I'd packed up to take to Ruijerd's house and sat down on the chair.

"So, um...congratulations on your marriage, Norn... Wait, no. Your engagement?"

"Thank you."

Now that I thought about it, when Big Brother announced my marriage, lots of people congratulated me. But not Aisha.

"It feels, I dunno, strange that you're getting married."

"You came here to say that?"

"No, um... Norn, what's it like? Getting married?" Aisha wouldn't look at me. She kept her eyes averted, as though she was asking something she wasn't supposed to.

"What do you mean?"

"Why are you going through with it?"

Ah. That's right. Now I remembered. Had it been Aisha who'd said it to me?

Why do you bother when you know you've got no talent?

My little sister never changed. I'd come to realize that her words that had seemed cruel when we were little were actually something else. She was good at everything, so she didn't understand how it felt.

No, actually, I was being too generous. When we were little, there probably was some cruelty behind it; that was why I couldn't stand her back then. But lately, I'd gotten over it.

When had Aisha stopped being unkind to me...? Was it when I'd become student council president? No, maybe it had been earlier... I wasn't sure exactly when, but she'd changed a lot since Lucie was born.

"I'm not sure what to say... For one thing, this marriage serves a purpose. And I love Ruijerd."

"What do you mean by 'love?'"

"It's like...I just find myself wanting to be with him, and when I see him, I want to hold him. That sort of thing."

"I love Big Brother. Is that a different love?"

"I... I'm not you, Aisha, so I can't say."

"I guess not..." Aisha stretched her legs out, then flopped down on the bed. "I just don't get it... Linia and Pursena keep going on and on about marriage lately.

Saying I missed my chance, or how now I've waited this long, I can't just settle. Is marriage worth getting that worked up about? I'm not sure. I mean, logically, I know I should want it, but it's not like everyone thinks that deeply about it, right?"

"Aisha, do you not want to get married?"

"I don't know."

"There isn't anyone you have feelings for?"

"No. When I was little, I thought I'd marry Big Brother, but that's different, somehow. But I can't even imagine leaving this house..."

Aisha had been glued to Big Brother ever since she was little. I first met her in Millis a little while after our father got back on his feet and started a respectable job. I hadn't been able to think of her as my little sister back then. I heard about people getting remarried to a partner who already had children from my friend in the dormitory, and I think it felt sort of like that. It didn't help that Lilia had treated her less like my little sister and more like a sort of junior maid. When did I begin to see her as my sister? Maybe it was when we went to school together in Millis or during our journey to Sharia with Ruijerd and Ginger. Either way, by the time we began living here in Sharia, she was my little sister.

"How do you feel right now?" Aisha asked.

"...Happy."

"Happy? How so?"

"It's hard to put into words. I guess it feels like I'm not worried about anything. I know that it won't be perfect, but without question, there will be good things."

As I finished speaking, Aisha sat up and stared intently at me. "*That's* happiness?"

"Hm...?"

"I mean, I feel like that pretty much all the time."

"That means you're happy all the time then, doesn't it?"

Aisha fell back on the bed again. "Eh... No, I don't think so. I'm kind of envious. I feel like I finally lost to you at something."

"It wasn't a competition!"

"Nope, I lost. I think I lost to you, Norn."

In the whole of my life, I had never beaten Aisha at anything. It wasn't just Aisha either. I never did especially well at school. My win rate in mock battle magic tests was 45 percent, and even though I tried my best, my average test score was only around 80. I never got anywhere near being top of my class.

If we were to compete in something I'd studied but she hadn't, I might be able to win once or twice, but after ten or twenty rounds, she'd win every time. Aisha was clever: she learned fast, and she could get straight to the heart of things. But now, she'd finally lost at something, and yet, I didn't feel very pleased. Besides, it wasn't as though we were in competition—I wasn't getting married to beat Aisha.

"Hey, Norn?"

"What is it?"

"After you get married, can I still come see you?"

That was unexpected, too. It had felt like Aisha was keeping her distance from me, though she didn't show it when looking after Big Brother's children. It was just that, when I was alone, she never approached me or talked to me unless she needed something.

"Yes, of...of course."

"If you have a baby, let me hold it, okay?"

"I will."

A baby...

I'd asked Sylphie all sorts of questions. Although it was probably too soon to be thinking about it, I assumed it would happen one day, and so I wanted to be prepared. Even now, Aisha looked after Big Brother's children. Sylphie said she was a great help. When I left this house, I'd have to raise my children all by myself. Yet another thing to worry about. Could I really manage...?

Sylphie reassured me I'd be fine, and Roxy fretted along with me. Eris would probably say "They just raise themselves" or something. Even so, it worried me.

"If anything, I'd be grateful if you could teach me what I don't know about raising children."

"You bet!"

"Thank you," I said, followed by a laugh. I was so glad to see Aisha return a smile.

Aisha and I carried on chatting late into the night. None of it was especially significant, just an endless stream of idle complaints that didn't reach any conclusion.

The next day, I took my belongings and moved to Ruijerd's house.

Rudeus

NORN AND RUIJERD'S WEDDING took place in the Superd village, and was done in their style. On the night of the full moon, the villagers came, each bearing food, then they all ate together to celebrate the new bride and groom. I wasn't a villager, but naturally, I brought a plate of food and the whole family with me. We were Norn's family. I wasn't taking "no" for an answer. Not that anyone tried—on the contrary, they were very welcoming.

Lilia and Aisha had made the food. Aisha seemed to have some seriously complex feelings about Norn's marriage. Ever since it was decided, I'd seen her get in trouble with Lilia countless times for loafing on the sofa, lost in thought. And a few days before the wedding, Aisha and Norn had stayed up late talking about something in Norn's room. Wonder what that was about?

Anyway, Aisha probably had a lot on her mind. It wasn't like she was unhappy for her sister or anything. In making the food for the wedding, she hadn't been stingy—if anything, she'd given it her all. She hunted down ingredients from Millis and Asura to make an enormous fruit cake. I wasn't sure if the Superd liked sweet food, but Roxy gave it her seal of approval. Then again, Roxy had a sweet tooth...

This was the happiest day of Norn's life, so the whole family came. That meant not only Arus, Sieg, and the little kids, but also Leo, Dillo, and Byt. Orsted wasn't family, but he was the one who'd set up the match, so he observed from a quiet corner. I also invited Norn's friends in Sharia, and they enthusiastically accepted. When Norn's junior school friends from the student council heard she was getting married, they bowed to me and begged for an invite.

I did feel a little sorry for the huddle of trembling humans surrounded by a crowd of Superd in the square, but once they saw how happy Norn looked, their nerves began to settle. By the time the feast began, they had fully gotten into the swing of things and lined up to pour Norn drinks.

She really did look happy. When she was at home—or rather, when she was with me—she usually looked sulky. For the entire time she was sitting beside Ruijerd, she beamed, albeit a little shyly. Every now and then, she would look his way, and he, sensing her gaze, would look back, at which Norn would blush and look down. Wearing a traditional bridal garment that the Superd women had made, with a table full of food before her, she glanced at her groom and blushed.

As a surprise, I also had a Millis-style ceremony slotted in partway through, which went over great. I had Norn and Ruijerd change into pure white. When they came back, Cliff—the surprise guest—stepped forward to give a Millis-style blessing. Ruijerd put the necklace I'd gotten ready in advance around Norn's neck and knelt, at which she, blushing furiously, placed a clumsy kiss on his forehead. Through the whole thing, Norn looked stunned, but when everything wrapped up, she wore a tearful smile. She was really, truly happy.

"Norn sure looks pretty, huh?"

That was Aisha. Whether it was the clothes making her beautiful or her happiness, I wasn't sure. Aisha gazed at her sister with envy.

"That'll be you one day, Aisha."

"No, it won't," she replied curtly. So Aisha wasn't planning on getting married. I personally wanted to see Aisha off too, just like I had Norn... Oh, well. Marriage wasn't all there was to life. I didn't mind her staying at home.

Man, Norn was a bride. It was enough to get me all choked up. When I first met her in Millis, she was tiny and ready to fight. There was even a point when she holed up in her dormitory room after starting school. As a kid, people thought of Norn as a handful, no good, clumsy. Then she joined the student council, carried out her duties as student council president commendably, and won the admiration of the junior students.

And now, she was married.

"*Sniff.*" My nose was suddenly stuffy.

Dear Paul,

Norn has grown up into a good and beautiful girl. Are you watching? No way you wouldn't be, right? If not, hurry and get over here.

"Don't cry, Big Brother."

"Crying? Me?"

"Yes, you. Rather than just sobbing in a corner, go talk to Norn."

"M-mm..."

The guests were lined up to give their congratulations to the newlyweds. The Superd didn't have a custom like that, but maybe Cliff had said something. Norn beamed as she thanked them all. Oh, it was joyful. Was it really all right for me to barge in there? I felt like I'd ruin it.

"You don't think Norn will be annoyed?"

"Not a chance."

"I dunno..."

"Well, I do."

I hesitated. "Will you come with me, Aisha?"

"No reason why not."

It wasn't like I was that worried about her. If anything, it was me I was worried about. I was absolutely going to sob. I was going to cry on the happiest day of Norn's life. I'd be a bawling, snotty mess, and everyone would point and say Norn's older brother was a big crybaby.

Would that be so terrible? Yes. Just the other day, Ruijerd had told me not to cry, so I wanted to hold it together. I wanted to at least get home first so I could cry with my face buried in Sylphie's lap.

"Okay," I said. "Let's go, then."

I just couldn't miss out on this moment with Norn. So, with the others in tow, I approached her.

"Oh." When Norn saw us, her lips went tight for a second. Almost at once, she was smiling again, but it seemed like maybe she'd wanted to say something.

Now I'm scared...

While I wavered, Sylphie overtook me to get to Norn first.

"Congratulations on your marriage, Norn."

"Thank you, Sylphie."

"It's work, but it'll be rewarding. Be sure to talk through your troubles and try your hardest."

"I will."

Sylphie smiled at Norn, then stepped aside. Next in line was Eris.

"Congrats, Norn!"

"Thank you, Eris."

"Don't slack off on your sword training, got it? Ruijerd's tough, but it's your job to have his back."

"I'll be sure to remember."

Eris nodded with satisfaction, then stepped aside. Next, she went over and started saying something to Ruijerd. It sounded like "If you don't protect Norn, I'll break you." That was our Eris.

Roxy came forward from behind Eris. "Congratulations, Norn."

"Thank you, Miss Roxy."

"No need to keep calling me 'Miss'... Well, all right. It's the last time, so let me say one more thing as your teacher. When you marry someone from a different race, I expect people around you will have more thoughts on it than you yourselves. Ignore them. Just go on as usual, and everyone will accept you eventually."

"Th-thank you, Miss Roxy!"

After Roxy came Lilia and Zenith. "Congratulations, Miss Norn."

"Lilia, Mother... Thank you."

"I think I may not have been a positive presence in your life, Miss Norn. All those times that Aisha made you unhappy, that was all my fault..."

"Don't say that. Lilia, you've been another mother to me. Aisha is my little sister. Yes, there were some bad things, but that was just life. It wasn't because of you, Lilia."

"You're... You're too kind..." Then she hiccupped. As she stood there all proper, Lilia immediately burst into tears. Literally everything seemed to make Lilia cry these days. Zenith patted her, making soothing sounds, but after a while, she turned her attention to Norn.

"Mother?" Norn said, but Zenith was silent. With a small smile, she took Norn's hand in both of hers, holding it tenderly, as though it were something precious.

"Mo... M-Mother..." Norn stammered. Zenith said nothing, but it was impossible to mistake her feelings. Tears began to pour down Norn's cheeks. Just like that, I knew her expression before had been her holding back tears.

"M-Mother, thank you... Th-thank you...for everything..." Norn was barely coherent. By the time my turn came around, her face was covered in tears and snot. Even though it was her wedding—the happiest day of her life...

"Big Brother..."

For the time being, I pulled out a handkerchief and put it to Norn's nose.

"C'mon, big blow."

"I can do it myself," Norn protested as she snatched the handkerchief and blew her nose. She looked unsure what to do with the handkerchief, so I tucked it back into my pocket.

Then, I faced Norn once more. "I, uh... Norn... Congratulations."

"Big Brother..." Norn looked up at me, her mouth set in a line.

What should I say? I could've sworn I had something ready, but my head's empty.

When I hesitated, Norn said, "Big Brother, um, thank you for everything. I...right now, I'm so happy. And it's all thanks to you, I know it is."

She told me she was happy, but that was clear just by looking at her.

"No, no... It's because you've done your best."

"I haven't done anything. Even the wedding was thanks to you!"

"Norn, if you hadn't been doing your best, Ruijerd would never have asked for your hand."

To Ruijerd, you were either a child or a warrior. If she hadn't changed, he never would have seen her differently.

"Still, thank you." Norn looked like she might cry again, so I reached into my pocket for the handkerchief. Just as I realized it was all damp, another one was suddenly held out from beside me—it was Aisha. I took her handkerchief and wiped away Norn's tears.

"Norn."

"Yes?"

"Um, I don't know what to say, and everyone's already said the important stuff, so there's not much left."

"Yes?"

"There'll be struggles and pain ahead for you, but...do your best for me to...to always be happy."

Funnily enough, I didn't cry—I'd been sure I would. Just like before, I started choking up, but the tears themselves had retreated. Standing there in front of Norn, all I felt was pride.

"I... I will!" Norn's tears stopped, and she beamed at me.

And so, Norn was married. Their height difference was almost as big as their age difference, but it seemed they were surprisingly compatible anyway. A year later, Norn had a baby. She was Norn's spitting image, but with green hair, a cute tail, and a gem on her forehead—a Superd girl. They named her Luicelia Superdia.

The face Orsted made when he heard it was terrifying to behold—he was *smiling*. But I understood. The name Orsted remembered and the name Norn and Ruijerd had chosen were the same.

Lucie and Dada

Mushoku
Tensei
redundant
reincarnation

CHAPTER 1
Lucie's First Day of School (Part 1)

THE DAYS SLIPPED BY. Eris and Roxy safely gave birth to their children, both girls. We named Roxy's daughter Lily and Eris's daughter Christina. I now had four daughters and two sons. The house was starting to get cramped; maybe it was time to start looking at an extension...and consider some family planning.

On top of that, Lucie turned seven, old enough to become an elementary school student. Elementary school—where children of the same age spent their days together, learning the fundamentals.

Truth be told, parents could handle teaching the basic knowledge. With school, the point was socialization. People need people. Some have the strength to make it alone, but they're the exceptions. School is where we learn how to make friends, how to relate to others, how to handle fights well. Here in the Ranoa Kingdom, there was no such thing as an elementary school, which wasn't a surprise, given there was no compulsory education.

If you ask me, kids ought to go to school. I was a dropout in my former life, but in this life, school had given me everything. I'd befriended Zanoba, I'd met Cliff and Badigadi and Nanahoshi and Ariel...and I'd married Sylphie. Without a doubt, it was my time at the Ranoa University of Magic that had allowed me to build my current rich personal life, and I wanted the same opportunities for every child.

When I'd announced that at the family meeting last year, the majority had been in my favor. Sylphie, Roxy, and Lilia were on my side, and although Eris had said, "They don't really need to go," she hadn't been strongly opposed. Thus we decided that from the age of seven, our children would attend the Ranoa University of Magic. I figured even if some of their classmates were older, it'd be a benefit.

Today was Lucie's first day of school. She would go for seven long years, more if she failed a grade, and this was Day One.

"Lucie, do you have everything?"

"I'm fine!" Lucie stood in the entranceway, her oversized school uniform hanging off her and her backpack too big for her body. Everything she had was brand new, including the beginner's staff and robe, the magic textbooks, and the lunchbox in her backpack.

Lucie inspected herself in the full-length mirror, apparently pleased with her shiny new getup. She had a smug smile on her face. Maybe that was why she sounded so nonchalant. We'd checked that she had everything over and over the previous night, and it wasn't like she had that much stuff to take in the first place. Yeah, she was probably okay.

Another check wouldn't hurt, though.

"Do you have your handkerchief?"

"It's in my pocket!"

"Do you have your pencil case?"

"It's in my bag!"

"And your lunchbox?"

"My bag!"

"What about a goodbye kiss for Daddy?"

"No way!"

No way?! Hm, what was left? Things you're likely to forget. Dreams for the future, hope, truth...

"Rudy, she said she's ready." Sylphie tapped me on the back, cutting through my thoughts. "She's growing up, she'll be fine."

Growing up... Oh, no. She was already seven. Seven meant she was a big kid—look how capable she was!

She's a big kid now.

"I'm fine, Dada! I'm gonna do my best!" Lucie said, making a fist. The gesture was courageous, adorable, and made me extremely anxious. If I were a kidnapper and I saw a tasty morsel like her, I'd gobble her up. She may have grown up, but she was still so tiny.

"Lucie, you mustn't go anywhere with anyone you don't know, okay?"

"Okay!"

"If anyone tries to force you to go with them, you shout your name really loud, understand?"

"Okay!"

"If they cover your mouth and say they'll kill you if you scream, you show them the letter Dada gave you and have them read it, understand?"

"Okaaay!"

The letter, by the way, contained my message to any kidnapper. It explained the nature of the person I served and the kinds of people I was connected with, and it went on to describe what would happen if any harm should come to Lucie. The kidnapper might not be able to read, so I'd also brought the matter to the slave traders in advance to ask them to ostracize anyone who kidnapped a child of mine. Any criminal who touched my daughter would be blacklisted from criminal society. Even then, I found fuel for my anxiety everywhere—I couldn't foresee everything, after all. I was beside myself with worry about what could happen.

"Lucie, you tell the teacher if any of your school friends bully you."

"Okay."

"I'm sure they won't, but if your teacher bullies you, you tell Blue Mama or the vice principal. They'll both be in the staff room."

"Okay."

"If you feel like you can't talk to Blue Mama or the vice principal about it, there's White Mama, or Red Mama, or Auntie Aisha, or Lilia, or Auntie Elinalise, or...well, the point is, tell someone. You can talk to Dada too, of course, or Dada's friends. Don't keep it to yourself."

"Okaaay."

"Also, if you think another kid is being bullied..." At this point, someone grabbed me by the collar and dragged me away.

I looked around and saw Sylphie glowering at me. Lucie, meanwhile, looked a bit dejected.

"Dada, I'll be fine..." she said, a little uncertainly, glancing up through her eyelashes. Had I scared her? Should I have sugar-coated it? "You go make a hundred friends," that sort of thing?

But this was important. Bullying could make you feel like no one would help you, but you always had someone on your side somewhere.

"Rudy, trust Lucie a little more," Sylphie said.

After a long pause, I said, "All right."

Right, of course. You send kids to school to make them more independent. It was no good trying to fix everything for her. Lucie would have to fend for herself someday. That was a long way off, of course, but independence was the whole point of school—that was what we'd decided as a family.

"Lucie, say bye-bye to everyone."

"Bye-bye!" Lucie called. She opened the door and bounded outside. Calling after her to take care, I watched her go.

There to see her off were me, Sylphie, Eris, Leo, Lilia, and Zenith. Roxy had already left for school. Aisha had left early—apparently, there'd been a problem with the mercenary band. The other kids were still snoozing.

"I'm gonna go train," said Eris.

"I'll start on the laundry," said Lilia.

"Time to clean," said Sylphie.

Everyone dispersed to attend to their chores, but I remained, staring at the door. Leo stayed with me. I bet he felt just like I did—worried. For all I knew, Lucie might have lost her way. She was supposed to have walked to the school with Sylphie and Roxy loads of times, but today, she was by herself.

I was worried. Maybe it was a bad idea to let a seven-year-old walk by herself. A sweet little girl like that shouldn't walk alone. I should have given her an entourage of tough-looking bodyguards, including a certain green-haired, white spear-wielding guy who likes kids.

And then there were classes. Lucie had enjoyed a gifted and talented syllabus from Sylphie, Eris, and Roxy. She wouldn't struggle to keep up, but she might get too far ahead and end up isolated. Not that we knew for sure she was special. Vice Principal Jenius had suggested it, but I wanted her to have a totally normal experience, so I'd enrolled her as an ordinary student. I made her take the exam too. She got an excellent score, but maybe that wouldn't translate to class. I worried that I was treating her like an experiment.

"Leo."

He replied with a quick bark when I called him, looking up as if to tell me there was no need to say more. We were on the same wavelength. Between us, no words were needed.

"Rudy! Don't even think about it!" Sylphie's sharp voice called from behind me as I put a hand on the front door. I turned and saw her with her hands on her hips, glaring at me.

"You promised me yesterday that we wouldn't intervene, remember?!"

"No, it's Leo. He wants to go for a walk."

At this, Leo turned away from me, then padded off down the corridor to the children's room. That traitor! He'd protect my children from outside enemies, but he wouldn't protect me from my own wife!

"Look, Rudy..." As I stood there rooted to the spot, Sylphie sighed, her hands still on her hips. "I believe it was being apart from you that allowed me to grow as a person. You taught me magic and how to study, and that gave me the foundation to stand on my own two feet. I was well set up when I was with Lady Ariel after the displacement incident."

"Mm."

"I agree it is important to teach and protect her, but she can't just have everything handed to her. Unless she makes her own discoveries and tries to figure things out for herself, she'll never find her own way."

I'd been looking forward to today. I planned to go to school with Lucie as her guardian, say hello to her teacher, then show her around the school. I even took today off just for that. But then Sylphie came to me yesterday and insisted—Lucie would go to school by herself.

"Just wait and see how she does for now, okay? Let her make her own mistakes."

"Yeah," I said at last. Sylphie could be persuasive. She'd spent seven years raising Lucie and watching over her. If she could confidently send Lucie off, then I ought to trust her judgment.

I really couldn't do everything for Lucie. I mean, I knew I was worrying too much. Lucie was a good kid. She took good care of her brothers and sisters, she was obedient, and from what I heard, the neighborhood children admired her too. If anything, she'd probably have a way easier time settling into school than I ever did.

So there was only one thing I could do: pray that she had fun at school. My prayers ought to reach my god, given that the god was also at the school.

"In that case," I said, "I'll head to work."

"Got it. If anything happens, I'll handle it. Okay?"

All the same, I felt somehow lonely as I headed for Orsted's office.

"—and that's what happened," I said, having recounted the events of the last hour. This was met with silence. "There's no doubt that Sylphie's right. For me, and for her too, it was being away from our parents that allowed us to grow. That goes without question."

I was venting. I *had* been persuaded—Sylphie and I had come to a decision as a couple. Luckily for me, the magic university had lots of people I knew and not much danger. From what I heard, Norn's zealous work with the student council had really straightened the place up. Under Aisha's leadership, Ruquag's Mercenary Band had grown, which straightened the whole town out as well.

But despite all that, I couldn't help but worry. It was a vague unease I couldn't put into words.

"Lucie's only seven, you know? Sending her to school alone, when she's still so small... I mean, yeah, I was seven when I went to live with Eris, and yeah, I was wandering around all over the village when I was five or so...but I still think we should at least drop her off and pick her up. What do you think, Sir Orsted?"

Orsted glowered silently. It was a face that said, "What does this have to do with work?"

Maybe I'd gone to the wrong guy for advice. Now that I thought about it, Orsted was my boss, so not the person to complain to about this sort of thing. It probably would have been all right if it were related to the Man-God, but family problems were not something he wanted to hear about. He probably didn't even know what to say. Heck, Lucie didn't even exist in the version of history Orsted knew... All the same, I somehow felt like Orsted would understand my torment.

Just as I thought this, Orsted stood up, looking like he was about to start a fight. Of course, I knew better. He wouldn't get mad over a thing like this. Pissing off Orsted would take more than that.

"You fool."

Wait, what? He's angry?

Oh, that was unexpected. Was I in trouble?

"Use this." Orsted handed me a black helmet. It was a spare of the one he used to mitigate the effects of his curse. What did he want me to do with it?

"You are not worried about your daughter, you merely want to go and see her, don't you?"

Oh! Of course! That was it!

I wanted to see her. It wasn't about whether I was worried or not. Well, of course it was about being worried, but also, I wanted to see her introducing herself to the class, to see her hand shoot up to answer the teacher's question, to see her standing on tip-toes to reach a book in the library... All those firsts.

The magic university didn't have observation days. I'd wanted to see Norn at school too but hadn't been able to. I wanted to see Lucie, at least.

"B-but if I go, Sylphie will be mad at me for sure," I said. Without a word, Orsted took off his coat, then hung it around my shoulders. It was as if he was telling me to use it. First the helmet, now this. What did he want me to do?

"Um. What's this for?"

"*You* cannot go."

I don't know what you're getting at. Please say it in a way that a fool like me can understand. Could we please take a break from the mind games?

"Hm?"

Hold on. So that's the idea, then? If Rudeus must not cross the bridge, then Rudeus *needn't go.*

You are what you wear. Change the clothes, change the man.

I wore a gray robe and was Orsted's right hand. That was my position. What if I was in a black helmet and a white coat?

I put on the helmet, then shrugged on the coat. The helmet was heavy, and the coat was thick and still warm. No doubt wearing it for too long would give me stiff shoulders, but it'd be worth it.

I went to stand in front of the mirror.

"Is that...me?"

There was no mistaking the person in the mirror: Dragon God Orsted!

Of course! With the black helmet and white coat, I could be the Dragon God! I'd get in trouble for going, so Orsted would go instead!

Hmm. Except, no. It just wasn't the same. I didn't look anything like Orsted. It was the height and the breadth of my shoulders. My whole vibe was wrong—I didn't have that strange aura of power that radiated off of him. The guy in the mirror was a total sham—I wouldn't pass.

"Hmm... Don't you think people will see through this?" I asked.

"They only need not know it is you."

Good point. I didn't have to be Orsted, I just had to not be me. In which case, honestly, just the helmet would do the trick. Sir Orsted really was brilliant.

"Sir Orsted," I said. "Thank you."

He grunted, then sat down in his chair again with a long-suffering air. Was he going to get back to sorting paperwork? Maybe I'd interrupted him. I was supposed to have had today off, after all.

"I'll be going then," I said. Still dressed as Orsted, I dashed out of the meeting room. There was no time to lose. To the university of magic, with all haste!

I left Orsted's office. The weather was gorgeous. The sky was blue; perfect for Lucie's first day of school. Maybe it was the outfit, but I felt somehow more powerful. This must have been how the donkey in the lion's skin felt. Right now, I felt like I could wipe the floor with the North God with the tip of my pinky finger.

"Are you going out, Sir Orsted?"

I froze.

Someone called out to me from the shadow of the office. I looked over and saw Alexander Rybak, North God Kalman III. No way! He hadn't read my mind, had he?

Wait, it's not like that. When I said I felt like I could wipe the floor with you, it was the same as like, I dunno, how you feel invincible after watching a boxing movie. You wouldn't hit a guy with glasses, right? I'm just an NPC!

"Where are you going today, Sir Orsted? Shall I accompany you?"

What could I say to that? I thought he was messing with me, but Alec's eyes were clear, and he spoke with sincerity.

"Oh, and thank you for the other day. To think that the North God Style four-legged stance had that advantage... I never imagined you would be so knowledgeable about North God Style. I have so much to learn. When I remember what I was like in the Biheiril Kingdom, I'm embarrassed."

There was no way he really thought I was Orsted, right? Alec had been at Orsted's side constantly these days. He *lived* in the basement of the office and padded around like he was Orsted's guard dog. Did he really not know his own master?

"You haven't noticed?"

"Noticed what?!"

But wait, he was North God Style. He could be trying to trick me. Like the Death God's Enthralling Blade—the technique he used to mislead his opponent.

"Tell me the truth. You know, don't you?"

At first, Alec stared blankly, but his expression quickly turned serious. He put his hand on his chin, then cocked his head to one side and frowned. You could practically see the question mark hovering above his head. He didn't have the slightest clue—I knew that face from dealing with Eris.

If it was an act, it was amazing, though.

"Forgive me," Alec said. "I'm slow, so I don't know what you mean."

"Seriously? You see there's something different, right?"

"Something small, I suppose? I'm not good at picking up on small details—I can't even avoid traps. I know it's unacceptable, but it's my flaw..."

Did he really not see it, then? I was a different height, a different build, and we sounded nothing alike. The helmet only weakened the effect of the curse, so if I were Orsted, Alec should at least have been feeling uncomfortable...

Is this for real?

At last, I said, "You'll find the answer in the CEO's office."

"I see! Thank you, Sir Orsted." Alec disappeared cheerfully into the office. I'd thought he was a bit sharper when I fought him in the Biheiril Kingdom. What changed? Was this just what he was like outside of battle? That would make sense, seeing as my own powers of concentration changed outside of battle. Maybe it was something like that.

All the same, I wasn't totally happy about leaving him at Orsted's side anymore... But right now, Lucie was more important than that.

Alec's response had demonstrated that, at least from a distance, you couldn't tell that I was Rudeus.

When Alexander entered the office, Faliastia at the reception desk met his eyes. When she saw him, she hesitated for a moment, wondering whether to ask her question or not, then opened her mouth.

"Erm, Sir Alexander?"

"What is it, Falia? I am on my way to the CEO's office for an answer, so please be brief."

"Sir Rudeus left dressed like Sir Orsted... Does he have some mission?"

Alexander blanched.

"Uh... Sir Rudeus? Dressed as Sir Orsted...?!"

Such a possibility had not occurred to Alexander. As far as he was concerned, the idea of dressing up as Orsted was so terrifying it was impossible. Why had Rudeus been dressed up as Orsted?

Well, that was obvious. He was clearly off to do something that required him to look like Orsted. Probably acting as a decoy or something. By dressing up like Orsted, he would lure out an enemy and keep them occupied while Orsted achieved a secret objective. That meant this enemy had to be someone formidable that only Orsted could face. Was it the as-yet-unseen Great Power, the Technique God? Or Death God Randolph, who was still a source of painful memories for Alexander? It might even be Armored Dragon King Perugius of the Three Godslayers. Or could it be Alex, North God Kalman II, Alec's own father? Any one of them would be too much for Rudeus to take alone. If he donned that Magic Armor of his, he would probably win, but then he would be no use as a decoy.

Alexander knew how brave Rudeus was. Rudeus, who knew no fear. His combat ability was, Alexander knew, less than his own, but the brilliance with which Rudeus had fought in the Biheiril Kingdom was burned in Alec's memory. It was the strength to face down something more powerful than yourself past the point of good sense. Alexander knew what to call it—courage. Atoferatofe had recognized that when she named him a champion. He had also realized something: this was his answer.

"Falia, please keep quiet about this."

"A-all right..."

The tilt of Faliastia's head gradually increased, but, paying her no mind, Alec reached for the door to the CEO's office. In his heart, he cradled the hope that Orsted would grant him the honor of fighting alongside a champion.

It was scarcely a few minutes later that Alexander would get his "answer" from Orsted.

CHAPTER 2
Lucie's First Day of School (Part 2)

AS MUCH AS POSSIBLE, I used the back roads. Even then, I felt like the disguise was drawing attention, but it was all in my head. Generally speaking, people aren't that interested in other people—unless they're dressed like Orsted, I guess, because I really was getting a few glances. That was only natural. Some time had passed since Orsted set up his offices on the outskirts of this town. Not many people had seen him, but they generally knew what he looked like. To them, someone wearing this black helmet and white coat could only be Orsted. Given I didn't have the curse, maybe "he" was leaving a good impression.

In that case, maybe I could try the main street. I could do good deeds to improve Orsted's image, like I had with Dead End. The main street was closer to the school too.

"Yeah, let's do it." It was two birds with one stone. If Orsted's reputation improved, it would work out in my favor too. *Oh, I got an idea!* I could suggest we hold a "Dragon God Festival." Everyone would dress up in white coats and helmets and party all night.

With that thought brewing in my mind, I headed for the main street.

"Wha?!" I spun around to duck into a shadow. A redhead I knew well had appeared on the main street. She was leading a big white dog with two children on its back along for the ride. It was Eris and Leo. Riding on Leo's back were Lara and Arus.

Leo, you disloyal mutt. After weaseling out of a walk with me, now you're out with Eris?

Well, okay. With me, it was different. I was pretending to go for a walk for my own selfish reasons, but Eris and Leo were patrolling the perimeter, going for a real walk.

Anyway, I was in a pickle. I hadn't thought I'd run into Eris here. But hey, this was Eris—maybe we could be in cahoots on this thing.

Hmm. How would I explain my outfit, though? She wouldn't suddenly draw her sword on me, would she? Besides, I had to consider the kids. I was blatantly doing something wrong—I was breaking my promise to Sylphie. Should I let them see me like this?

Absolutely not.

This really wasn't good. I was in disguise and everything.

Maybe I should go home after all... I'd come this far, but for a fleeting moment, I wondered if it wouldn't be better to just head home and wait for Lucie.

Hmmmm. Ahh, but I really did want to see Lucie on her big day. It was selfish; I knew that. It wasn't like what Sylphie had said. I wasn't doing this because I didn't trust Lucie. I wasn't here to help Lucie from the shadows.

I swear to God that I will not interfere. Not even if Lucie looks like she's going to cry.

Once she was home, I'd get the story from her. That's when I'd help her and give her advice.

Got that, Rudeus? That's the line. You cross it, you break your promise to Sylphie.

I'd made that up without consulting Sylphie, but so long as I stuck to it, I wouldn't be doing anything wrong. Of course, once this was over, I'd be sure to talk to her and apologize. "I was so desperate to see Lucie in class that I went," I'd say. "I couldn't restrain myself," I'd say.

Got that? You can handle that, right? You'll accept your scolding, yes?

I sure will!

All right! Good boy, Rudeus!

"Woof! Woof!"

Bah. Looked like Leo had noticed me. His nose was twitching and pointed in my direction.

"What is it, boy? What's up?" Eris was going to notice me too. It wasn't like it'd be a big problem if they found me, but explaining why I was dressed like this would take a while. I didn't feel like getting held up, so I'd have to take a detour.

"You, skulking back there! Show yourself now!" The thought came too late. Eris had already noticed me. This is what happened when you stood out...

Okay, what now? Did I show myself or not? And if I did, what did I say?

But wait, hm. They're still far away. At this distance, I might keep my cover.

I stepped halfway out of the shadows. Eris had a hand on the sword at her hip, and Leo wagged his tail. Then, my eyes met those of the two sitting astride Leo—Lara and, sitting with Lara's arms wrapped around him, Arus. They gaped at me with eyes full of innocence.

"Orsted...?" With a dubious look, Eris took her hand off her sword, at which I turned and walked away. Casual-like. We'd just happened to run into each other.

"Wait a minute," came Eris's voice after a moment.

"Tch...!" Was the game up? Eris was a Sword King; she'd be able to tell I wasn't Orsted at a glance, wouldn't she?

No sooner had I stopped than Eris said, "No, just my imagination. C'mon, Leo."

She turned away and started walking. Leo glanced back in my direction, but he didn't chase me.

All according to plan.

My eyes met Lara and Arus's. Lara looked dreamy and Arus was gaping—they were watching me. I imagined they were seeing me off.

I arrived at the school. Avoiding the main gate, I scaled a wall to slip inside, then headed for the classrooms. I'd attended classes for a few years, so I knew where the first-year classroom was. I set off toward it, staying out of the sight of the students who were between classes or taking their lessons outside in the sunshine.

Man, this place hasn't changed one bit.

It'd only been a few years, but the passage of time hit me hard. I didn't recognize most of these kids. I saw more elves, beastfolk, dwarves, and such around than there had been when I was a student. There were quite a few demons too.

Roxy told me over dinner one night that students with tics to the leaders of the elves and the dwarves were in the student council. With the voices and position of non-humans becoming more powerful, the number of students of other races enrolling from around the world increased. The school had never looked like this while Ariel was student council president. Despite their increased numbers, the other races were getting along well. That was probably Norn's legacy as student council president—she didn't stand for interracial discrimination. She'd left her mark on the culture of the place. Some of the nobles from the Magic Nations apparently wrinkled their noses at that, but personally, I was proud.

Lost in thought, I walked along the corridor. Then, just as I was about to turn a corner...

"Hm?"

"Ack."

I ran into the person who'd just come around it. They had five students in tow, or rather, five students clinging to them. "Clinging" sounded sort of unpleasant, but the gist of it is that they were popular. Given that the students were holding notebooks, presumably they were going over something from class they hadn't quite understood. Very admirable. Whatever they wanted to know, this person would have the answers. Her lips only spoke the truth. I mean, okay, sometimes there were mistakes, but those mistakes were the truth too.

You're all receiving divine revelation. Only her words hold that kind of power. Hear me, O students. Listen faithfully, give their meaning careful thought, and apply them to your lives. O students, in this moment you are truly blessed.

"Orsted...?" At last she spoke, sleepy eyes narrowing in suspicion before turning up to look at me. A few seconds passed, and then those eyes widened. "No, Rudy? Rudy, it's you, right? Isn't it?"

You couldn't get anything past Roxy. Her keen eyes could always find the truth.

"How...did you know?" I had to ask. I was a fool, and I had to know. I got it, all right? Roxy was brilliant. Sometimes, she probably just arrived at the truth without having to go on a whole journey to get there.

"The only one with the courage to pretend to be Orsted is you, Rudy."

Well, she wasn't wrong.

"Does Sir Orsted know about this?"

"Um, yes. In fact, it was Sir Orsted's suggestion."

"Really...? Then I suppose there has to be a good reason, right?" Roxy stared hard at me. It seemed she'd misunderstood me in just the right way.

Hmm. Was I going to deceive Roxy? Was I going to lie to her for a momentary attack of selfishness? Could I live with that? *Rudeus, how could you?*

"No, it's not a good reason." I could never lie to Roxy. Well, no. I might do it to save a life, but this was different. If I lied here, me from twenty years in the future would come swooping back in time to shoot a Stone Cannon at me. Or I'd lose my identity as I liquefied into a blob.

"Then why are you dressed like that?"

"I, um, I wanted to see Lucie..."

"Lucie?" Roxy echoed after a pause. "I thought you promised Sylphie?"

"I'm not trying to help her from behind the scenes or be an overprotective parent. I just, um, you know, Lucie in her lessons, I wanted to see her..." I mumbled. Roxy looked up at me. It was reproachful. The students around us weren't sure what to make of this situation between adults.

Forgive me, forgive me.

At last, Roxy's gaze softened, and she said, "All right. If you'll be sure just to watch and not offer her any help, I'll pretend I didn't see you. We'll say that Orsted came to inspect the university."

"Mistress...!" I gasped.

"Just this once, all right?"

"Of course. Once I get home, I'll apologize to Sylphie too."

"Very good."

God had forgiven me. I was in Roxy's debt. From this day forth, I would face Roxy and pay her the deepest obeisance five times a day.

"Now, I have to help these students with their studies before the next class, so... By the way, Rudy, do you know where Lucie's classroom is?"

"Yes, of course."

"All right then." Roxy gave my hand a quick squeeze, then walked off down the corridor. The students chased after her, asking, "Who was that?!"

She was a hit. Of course she was. She was my teacher.

"Right," I said, psyching myself up again. I set off down the corridor.

I arrived at the classroom. I tried to peek in from the corridor, but then I figured that was a bad idea, so I went around from the outside. If rumors spread that Orsted was spying on classrooms, it could affect the fortunes of the corporation. Thinking quickly, I made a partition screen near the classroom window so no one around me could see me. Then, through the window...

"Wait. What if I just went to observe the class and called it an inspection?"

Roxy had given me the green light. I could just ask. If I'd just explained the situation to someone like Jenius, he'd make it look official. I'd miscalculated. Oh, well. For now, I'd be happy just to see Lucie.

I opened up the Eye of Distant Sight and looked through the window. Rows of desks filled the classroom along with neat rows of first-year students, most of them adults older than fifteen. There were a few kids who looked around ten or so. Almost none were seven, and the ones who looked little were probably mostly dwarves. In addition to the ordinary humans, there were demons, elves, dwarves, and beastfolk. Some looked kind, some looked peaceful, some looked cheeky. A good variety. The ones sitting in the back of the classroom were hard-faced, probably former adventurers. They wouldn't bully Lucie if she got tangled up with them, would they? No, even that lot wouldn't bully a seven-year-old. Where was Lucie...? Ahah, there she was, right in the front. *That's my girl.*

The desk was so big it'd be hard for her to see over the front. That was a problem. She was listening to the teacher with a serious look on her face and taking notes, but she looked uncomfortable. It might be a good idea to have her take a cushion tomorrow. Beside her was a girl who looked about ten. Was she a dwarf? No, she seemed like a human. And from the way her hair was done up, likely a noble. Now and then she said something to Lucie, then stared at her magic textbook. Apparently, the custom of taking notes was unfamiliar to her. Serious-faced Lucie was pointing at the magic textbook and saying something. Maybe because she was whispering, I couldn't hear her. Maybe she was teaching her something. Had she already made a friend her age? Had she settled in?

Maybe because it was the first day of classes, the teacher didn't seem to be teaching them anything important. Based on what was on the blackboard, they were starting from the most elementary of elementary magic. Lucie had passed that years ago, so it was sure to be a piece of cake.

"Teacher!"

Just then, Lucie raised her hand.

"Yes?"

"I've heard that your mana capacity isn't the same all through your life, that it increases depending on how much you use magic as a child. I think what you're saying is wrong!"

What she was learning at the university and what Sylphie and Roxy had taught her didn't quite line up.

Lucie, sometimes it's better not to say these things. You won't find many teachers who're happy to be told they're wrong.

"What's your name?" the teacher asked.

"I'm Lucie. Lucie Greyrat."

"Greyrat...? You're from Miss Roxy's household, then?"

"I am!"

"Ahah. I see you've had an education!"

The teacher's eyes glittered. She wasn't going to disrespect my Roxy, was she?

No way they'd disrespect a parent in front of her daughter. I'd made up my mind to show restraint today, but tomorrow, all bets were off. *Better not walk in any dark alleys tomorrow, buddy.*

"It is true that such a theory is circulated by certain people, and perhaps it was so for your father and mother. It may also have been true for Miss Juliet. However, its veracity is, as of yet, unclear. Your father and mother and

Miss Juliet may simply have been special. It may be that it does not apply to demons and beastfolk. It may even be that your father and Miss Roxy have misunderstood something. There has not been sufficient testing, and I was not involved in the research. As such, I teach that one's mana capacity stays the same throughout one's life. That is how it was for me."

The teacher went on and on, either to convince Lucie or herself. Lucie listened seriously.

"From here on, you—all of you—will learn a great many things, both magic and otherwise. You will learn while you are at school, and you will go on learning after graduation. We are pioneers among magicians, and we will teach you a wide range of things. You may believe what we teach you or not—you are free to think for yourselves. You may claim we are wrong and prove as much. If you succeed in proving it, then it will be your turn to teach us. So, convince me."

Good, good. With that open-minded attitude, she seemed like she wouldn't be a bad teacher—she might even be a good teacher.

"That is all. Any questions, Lucie?"

"No! Thank you!"

"Good, then you may be seated. Let us get back to the lesson." The teacher smiled, and Lucie sat down. A round of applause rose up from around her. Lucie turned to look at her classmates behind her, startled, then looked down, her face beet red.

Don't worry, Lucie. You were correct. Forget whether it was really *correct—everyone who thought so clapped. You should be proud.*

Just then, the girl beside Lucie patted her on the head, then said something. Lucie looked up and grinned.

That's right, you be friends with my girl. You can fight, just so long as you're friends.

I went on watching Lucie's lessons for a while longer. Some of her teachers were good, some were bad. Lucie didn't hesitate to ask them questions and raise her doubts. The teachers sometimes answered and sometimes evaded; sometimes, they corrected Lucie's mistakes while going on with the lesson.

Lucie stood out. A seven-year-old girl with a keen mind for learning had to be a rarity. A crowd gathered around her at the lunch break as she ate from her lunchbox, and by evening, Lucie was the talk of the school. People gathered around her asking her all kinds of questions: about her parents, her family, where she lived, and about Lucie herself. A genuine celebrity. Some of those people probably knew she was my daughter and were trying to ingratiate themselves. That was fine. Every new person was a treasure. Even if a relationship started with selfish motives, you never knew where it'd end up. And it's a long life; it wouldn't hurt her to get to know a few bad apples.

"Phew." The final lesson ended. I was satisfied. It was only the first day, and Lucie was already settling into school life. Not that I'd been worried, of course. She was Sylphie's daughter. She, Roxy, and Eris had all given her a good education, so I had nothing to fear. Okay, well, if there was anything, it was that she was *my* daughter. She could easily have spent her first day in a seat on the edge of the classroom pretending to be asleep, but she hadn't pulled anything like that. She'd face challenges from here on out, but she'd be okay. Lucie would go to school every day and make lots of wonderful memories, and I'd listen to her tell me about them at the dinner table. I'd be able to enjoy my dinner with a smile.

Time to head home. But first, I'll give Orsted his coat and helmet back. With that, I lifted the Earth Wall spell I'd used for the partition screen.

"Oh." On the other side of the wall was a woman. She was slim, with white hair, and she wore comfy-looking pants and a sleeveless top. Her white arms emerged from her shoulders and extended down to where her hands were planted on her hips—and she looked annoyed.

It was Sylphie.

"Ahem... What seems to be the trouble?" I said, trying my very hardest to sound like Orsted.

"What are you doing here, Rudy?"

Oh, I was cooked.

"Oh, um... What brings *you* here, Sylphiette?"

"Lara said that she saw her father on her walk. She said your face was hidden, and you were dressed strangely."

"Oh... Right."

It was Leo. Leo had betrayed me! He hadn't used his eyes; he'd picked me up with his nose. My scent might have been mixed up with Orsted's, but if Leo said I was there, Lara would have figured it out, and Leo and Lara could talk. That explained it.

At length, Sylphie spoke again. "You *dressed up*." Her shoulders were trembling. That was anger. Sylphie was something else when she got angry. I couldn't explain exactly how, but when Sylphie was in a bad mood, it usually meant I was so totally in the wrong that the whole family was mad at me. It made life super uncomfortable. I might have to spend a week in the dog house.

"Do you really trust me and Lucie so little?" Sylphie started crying.

Shit. This is bad. This is worse than anger.

I got down on my knees. "No, it's not like that, not at all. I just wanted to see Lucie being brave. I wanted to see her shooting her hand up to ask questions in class and studying as hard as she could. I, you know, it's just, I haven't been around much, you know? To help raise Lucie."

When I'd stammered out my response, Sylphie looked at me, still crying.

"Really?"

"Really. I couldn't help myself. I was going to tell you about it once it was all over."

Sylphie regarded me for a moment, then said, "You're lying, aren't you?"

"It's the truth. I was going to apologize."

"You wanted to see Lucie's class that much?"

"Yes."

Sylphie held out a hand to pull me to my feet. Her tears had slowed. "Then I was in the wrong. You wanted to see her that much, and I forbade you from even getting a glimpse."

"No, you didn't do anything wrong. When you said it, I was convinced."

"Mm... Oh." As we stood there talking, Sylphie suddenly looked up with an expression that said, "Oh, no."

When I turned around, the reason became clear. "Ah..."

At some point, all the students in the classroom had turned to look out the window at us. That obviously included Lucie. She was staring at me and Sylphie, and she was irked.

"Today, I made friends with a girl called Belinda."

Sylphie and I walked home together with Lucie as a family. We walked in a row, each of us holding one of Lucie's hands. I'd thought Lucie would sulk over the fact that I'd come to school, but she didn't. It seemed she'd had all sorts of fun during her first day at school, and she told us about all of it, one by one.

"Belinda said she's the daughter of a Ranoan minister. She's little like me, but clever, so they let her start school. She said she wants to be the best in school and show her father what she can do."

"Wow, that's amazing."

"Oh, and my first lesson was with Blue Mama. Everyone made fun of her and I was so cross, but then Blue Mama, she said she'd do a little magic and that made everyone go quiet. Then she said, 'If you don't want to listen to my class, that's up to you!' She was so cool!"

"Let's tell Blue Mama that story at dinner. I'm sure she'll like it."

This wasn't what I'd planned, but this was nice. I squeezed Lucie's hand and walked side-by-side with Sylphie. It wasn't good to block up the street by walking in a row like this, but hey, who cared? This was my town.

"Did you have fun at school, Lucie?"

"Uh-huh!" Lucie replied, glowing. I had nothing to worry about.

"Hey, Dada? I *was* fine, wasn't I?" Lucie asked, like she'd read my mind.

"Yes, you were. You were great."

"Am I your girl, Dada?"

"Ha ha ha. I think you might be too amazing to be mine."

Lucie was a splendid young woman, no matter how you looked at it. She didn't need a guardian. Now, her dada, on the other hand, he wasn't fine at all. He *did* need a guardian.

"By the way, Rudy?" All of a sudden, Sylphie poked me.

"Huh?"

"How long are you going to keep that outfit on?"

I looked down at myself and remembered the thick white coat and the black helmet. I was still Shadow Orsted.

"I'll give them back tomorrow."

Yeah, tomorrow. Tomorrow would be fine. I hadn't said I'd return them today, and Orsted wasn't in a hurry as far as I knew. Man, the fabric of this coat was really nice… It felt similar to red dragon skin. Aisha would probably know what it was.

Just then, a question occurred to me. "By the way, Lucie?" I said. It was a small thing, just something I wanted to check.

"Yes, Dada?"

"Question: What color is Dada's hair?"

I didn't ask because I didn't trust Lucie. I just wanted to check.

"Brown!"

"That's right. You are clever, Lucie. I'll be expecting big things from you. Yes, that's my girl."

"Hmph, don't make fun of me!" Lucie said, pouting a little. Smiling at her, I arrived home happy.

"Only, Rudy? You broke your promise to me, so you'll have to go without for three days, okay?"

"Understood."

Okay, so I'd live like a monk for a few days, but I was still happy.

The next day, an odd rumor was going about town. People were saying that Orsted was after Lucie. I mean, it was probably because I'd walked around in that outfit. Rumors came and went. I knew they had no basis in reality, and so did Sylphie and the rest of the family, so I wasn't worried. And so, I went to return Orsted's coat. He gave me a scary glare, and I had to work hard to come up with an excuse to explain myself, but...that's a tale for another time.

CHAPTER 3

Lucie's Family

MY NAME IS LUCIE GREYRAT. I'm the oldest daughter in the Greyrat family. My family is big. I have three mamas, three sisters, three brothers, two grandmas, two aunties, and three pets. Thirteen people and three animals in all. So big!

First, I'll introduce my mamas. I have three. One has white hair, one has blue hair, and one has red hair. White Mama is the one who gave birth to me. She was my dada's first bride. She's the youngest of my mamas, and Dada says she needs the most attention. White Mama talks a lot. She says, "Making friends is important, and you must never bully the weak." She told me how important it is to value your friends.

Blue-Hair Mama is Lara's mama. She was Dada's second bride. She looks younger than my other mamas, but she's the oldest. Dada says she's the most reliable. Blue Mama didn't used to talk much, but she sometimes said, "Live the way you like, and if there's ever anything you don't understand, ask someone." There wasn't anything she'd taught me herself, but she knew everything and answered all my questions.

Red-hair Mama is Arus's mama. She was Dada's third bride. She looks the oldest of my mamas, but Dada says she's the most immature. Red Mama isn't very good with words, but she always told me, "Protecting someone—that's what's important. To do it, you have to be strong." She said that, and she trained me up.

I want to follow everything my three mamas taught me. I'll make friends, then I'll become strong so I can protect them. I will never bully the weak. If I'm in trouble, I'll ask Blue Mama what to do. If I do that, I can't go wrong, and they'll praise me. Dada will too. He'll say, "Aren't you clever, Lucie? You're such a good big sister."

I have four brothers and sisters. The oldest is my sister Lara. She's very kind. She has long hair the same color as Blue Mama's that she wears in one braid. She's kind of strange. She often talks to Blonde Grandma and our pet, Byt. Grandma and Byt don't speak, but Lara can talk to them. Maybe because she's always so out of it, kids tease her and pull her hair when we play in the square. I try to help her, but she doesn't look like she minds much. It's confusing.

She loves naps. She's always falling sound asleep on Leo's back.

My oldest brother is Arus. He's a brave boy. His hair is the same color as Red Mama's, but it's short. He's cheeky, but he always tries to look after me and Lara. I think he's doing what his mama taught him, just like I am. Red Mama thinks he can do anything. Lately, they do running and sword practice every day. Arus is best friends with Auntie Aisha. He looks happy whenever they're together.

My littlest brother is Sieg. He's a crybaby. When he chases after Arus, he cries when he gets left behind. I scold Arus every time. After that, he takes Sieg's hand and puts him on Leo's back. When Sieg tries to get up on Leo's back, Lara shifts back a bit and pulls him up in front of her. She holds on to him to make sure he doesn't fall off, then falls fast asleep.

I'm actually the only one who knows about it, but Sieg is super strong. He can pick up really heavy boxes without any problem.

I have another little brother called Clive. He's the same age as Lara, and he isn't actually my brother. He's

White Mama's Grandma's son. Mama says that he's like my cousin. I don't know what to call him, but he's my little brother. He comes to play at our house a lot, and he and Arus are friends. He's always hugging me. When I pat him on the head, he smiles like he's embarrassed.

My littlest sisters are Lily and Christina. They were only just born. They're tiny so I don't know what they're like, but they'll be good girls.

I'm the big sister to all of them. Because I'm the big sister, my mamas always tell me I have to be grown-up. And I am. My little brothers and sisters are all very good, and I want to protect them.

I have two grandmas too. Blonde Grandma is Dada's mother. Her name is Zenith. She's very pretty, but she doesn't talk, and she doesn't say anything if you talk to her. She's always in the garden with Byt, staring off into space. Whenever I'm sad or mad, she strokes my hair. She's a strange grandma.

Brown-Hair Grandma is Aisha's mother. Her name is Lilia. They say she used to work as a maid at Grandpa's house. She still acts just like a maid. My three mamas like her, but when I was little, I didn't understand how she could be my grandma. Once, on the street, I heard someone say, "The maid is your inferior. Order her around."

I tried it. Red Mama was nearby, and she got really mad at me. She spanked me until my bottom was bright red, then put me out of the house and told me to spend the night thinking about what I'd done. I sat huddled up against Leo until Brown-Hair Grandma let me back into the house. She explained what had happened to me. That was how I learned that she was a maid, but she was also my grandma, and I was not to order her around.

I also have two aunties. Both of them are still young, so they get angry when I call them "Auntie," and even though they *are* my aunties, they feel more like big sisters. My older auntie is Blonde Grandma's daughter and Dada's little sister. Her name is Norn. She always tries her very best, plays with me a lot, and teaches me lots of things. I love her. When I grow up, I'm going to be just like her. A little while ago she got married, so she moved away. She barely ever comes home, and when she does, she's always arguing with my younger auntie. It might look like they don't like each other, but sometimes they smile while they argue. I think they're playing.

My younger auntie is Brown-Hair Grandma's daughter. They have different mamas, but she's Dada's little sister. Her name is Aisha. She always wears maid clothes, just like Brown-Hair Grandma, and she runs the house.

Whenever I do anything around the house, she helps. She teaches me anything I want to know about cooking and washing. Mama says that she's good at everything. I heard she even helps Dada with work. For some reason, Brown-Hair Grandma sometimes gets mad at her. It's strange.

I have three pets. Leo is a big white dog and a guardian beast. He's really clever and understands what we say. He watches over everyone in the family, and Dada says that if I'm in trouble, I should go to Leo. Lara is his favorite, and when he's at home, he sticks to her like glue.

Dillo the Armadillo is Blue Mama's mount. He's timid, and when he's told off, he either rolls over to show his belly or curls up in a ball. When anything happens while we're out, he sometimes growls and scares off whoever it is. In his own way, he tries to protect us too.

Byt the Treant protects Auntie Aisha's vegetable garden. He's a plant monster, so I have no idea what he thinks about. He's often with Blonde Grandma and Lara. He has no mercy for anything that damages the garden's crops. He gets nutrients from the little birds he catches stealing Dada's favorite "rice." He's scary, but he's never hurt anyone in the family. When we get close, he opens the gate for us and gives us fruit from the trees. He's family too.

I have lots of people in my family. I have lots of mamas and lots of little sisters and brothers, but I only have one Dada. I really love Dada. I heard that when I was a baby, I used to avoid him, but now I don't. The way he smells makes me feel totally safe. Sometimes his beard gets scratchy, but I like that too. Dada doesn't let me touch his beard much. Sometimes it gets really shaggy, but when I try to touch it, he gently takes my hand and says, "Sorry, I'll shave it now, okay?" Then he heads for the bathroom. I don't know why, but I guess Dada wants to. I wish he'd let me touch his beard, but I like him anyway.

I feel like Dada doesn't think I can do a lot. I'm not sure why, but it's how I feel. He worries about me, and he loves me, but he thinks I'm really little.

I'm sure it's because Dada is so amazing. I don't know how he is, but everyone seems to think so. When he was my age, he could already do Saint-tier magic, and not only did he go to school, he ended up teaching. When I turned five and started to go out to play in the town and park, I started saying good morning to lots of different people. They all knew about Dada. The most important-looking people were the ones who praised him the most. My mamas are amazing too, but I've known since I was little that Dada is really special.

Dada...doesn't expect much from me, and I guess he doesn't from anyone. But I want him to praise me. I do what my mamas teach me, and I protect my little brothers and sisters. My mamas give me lots of praise for that. I want Dada to praise me too. I'm already seven. Today, I'm starting school. It's a school for grown-ups too, and it's where White Mama and Blue Mama and Dada all went. Red Mama didn't, but I heard she teaches sword fighting there sometimes.

Knowing you, Lucie, you'll be fine. Remember everything we've taught you and you'll do great. That's what Blue Mama told me. But I'm still nervous. Will I do okay in a place full of grown-ups? Will I make friends? I'm happy, but I'm nervous. I'm sure if I do my best, Dada will praise me. "Amazing, Lucie. That's my girl," he'll say. He'll have high expectations for me, I bet. I'm going to work hard to meet them.

The Seven Knights of Asura

Mushoku
Tensei
redundant
reincarnation

CHAPTER 1
Isolde Looks for a Husband

LONG, LONG AGO, back before Water God Style existed, there was a country terrorized by the Sea Dragon King. They had fished in the Sea Dragon King's waters and incurred its displeasure. Almost every day, fishing boats were ravaged, and Sea Dragons began to appear in the ports. Though the knights of that land tried to stand against it, the Sea Dragons were vast and glided through the water. They were strong, and rapidly wore down the kingdom's forces. Doom was nigh.

The matter weighed heavily on the king. He declared that he would give his daughter and his throne to anyone who slayed the Sea Dragon King. In response, many knights, champions, and heroes challenged the Sea Dragon King, yet all were defeated.

One day, a man appeared. A battered old sword hung at his hip, and his garb was ragged. Recent tales paint him as breathtakingly handsome, but in the truest retellings, he was no sight to behold—he looked like a vagabond, his face smeared with grime.

He went by the name Reidar. He presented himself to the king and asked if he might slay the Sea Dragon King. Naturally, the king said yes, though he had half lost hope and didn't have faith in this stranger.

But Reidar was strong. He froze the surface of the ocean to peer underneath into its depths, spying on the movement of the Sea Dragons. Then, quick as a blink, he closed on the Sea Dragon King. The Sea Dragon King smashed through the ice, writhing as it lashed out at Reidar. With his battered old sword, this brave soul turned aside its deadly attack, then struck back with a blow that lobbed the head right off the beast.

With the Sea Dragon King's head in hand, Reidar returned to the kingdom where a hero's welcome should have awaited him. Though the king lavished upon him enough gold and jewels that he need never work another day, that was all he received, for at the last minute, the king decided to withhold the hand of his daughter and his throne.

Reidar was not angry, but a great sadness came over him, for he was in love with the princess. As he watched her from afar at parades and ceremonies, she had won his heart. Though he knew he could have taken the throne by force if he so desired, Reidar decided that if he could not marry his beloved, he would leave this country.

Yet there was one who became angry in his place: the princess. She railed against the king, punching and kicking at him before storming out of the castle. She went after Reidar, catching up to him as he made to leave the country and throwing herself at his feet.

"I have given up my country. I am no longer a princess. I have no name. In making me yours, you will not gain a kingdom, nor will you become king. If that is acceptable to you, I beg of you—make me your wife."

With a smile, Reidar took the princess in his arms. Together, they left the kingdom. The pair were married, and they disappeared.

Years later, in some far corner of the world, the Water God Style was born. Or so it is said.

This episode was the basis for the law that states, "The Water God's companion shall forsake their name."

Isolde Cluel was the head of the Water God Style in Asura, as well as one of the sword instructors for the kingdom's knight order. At present, she was a Water Emperor, but she had only just learned the third of the Water God Style's five secret techniques. In a few months, there would be a ceremony in which she would take the name that declared her Water God.

Her age was unclear, but she looked to be in her twenties. She had aristocratic features and lovely hair so dark it was almost blue. Her beauty was plain to see, but some whispered that she used makeup to look younger. In the whole of Asura, the only person who knew her age was Queen Ariel.

Isolde was actively searching for a husband. When she became Water God, it would mean an end to many, many moons of strict training. From here on, she would continue to hone her skills, but it was a milestone, so she felt it was about time she thought about marriage.

Unfortunately, her search was not going smoothly. It wasn't that she lacked potential partners, of course. The Water-God-to-be was in demand, especially by Water God Style swordsmen. There was no shortage of men who were entranced by her beauty and impressed by her dedication to her training.

Yet they were swordsmen—they lived by the blade. Few were broad-minded enough to marry a woman who was stronger than they were. Isolde, for her part, would have preferred a man who was her equal, or at least someone with King-tier abilities. An Asuran nobleman would do, and women of the Water God Style were popular in Asura. Swordswomen of the defensive Water God Style, unlike their Sword God counterparts, were not overly assertive; they were soft-spoken and feminine. They could be confrontational at times, and they knew their own minds.

In Isolde's case, she knew how to conduct herself at court. She was young, pretty, good-natured, and would respect her husband. On top of that, she was a skilled swordswoman. There were many Asuran noblemen who'd have liked to make her their wife. They'd have her wait on them during the day and warm their beds at night. Needless to say, Isolde was not interested in a husband with only prurient interests.

But every now and then, she would meet someone and think, *He might do.*

He had good looks, a good nature, and a good pedigree, and he wasn't a bad swordsman. This charmer kept his perversions well-hidden and came up to her flashing a mouthful of pearly white teeth.

It was the prince. Isolde fell for him hard. She fell for him, even as the people around her told her, "Not him. That one's a scumbag when he can get away with it." The fact was, the prince was good-looking and friendly, and Isolde couldn't resist a pretty face. *He might do,* she thought. But when Isolde gave the prince a caveat, he retracted his offer of marriage without a second thought.

"One day, I will be Water God and take the name Water God Reida Reia. If you marry me, you must forsake your name and family. The Water God's companion may not have a family name."

This was the custom of the Water God. There was no penalty for failing to respect it, nor any benefit in doing so. It was simply the tradition of the Water Gods, including the former Water God Reida, who was Isolde's grandmother. Isolde's father had no family name, either. Cluel was her mother's name. As such, Isolde, who revered her grandmother, intended to respect the custom as well. But alas, the prince who had so royally reeled her in her was a noble. He had been born a noble and lived as one. His life was built on his family's rank. No one wanted to marry Isolde enough to forsake their name and family, no matter how much they liked her.

Isolde was worried. Several years had passed since she started looking for a husband. She'd had a few prospects, but always stumbled at the final hurdle. At this rate, she wouldn't find a husband before she took the Water God's name.

Yet Isolde had confidence in herself. She was well groomed, a great cook, and could put on makeup like an artist. She never skipped a day of hair and skincare. She liked to think she was an excellent speaker. Her Water God Style training had included the art of conversation—where you coaxed the other party into speaking first. She really was doing her best.

Despite all her efforts, however, she still couldn't find a husband. Eris had, even Nina had, but she somehow just couldn't do it. They'd both had childhood friends, and they didn't have any restrictive traditions to follow. Isolde had thought she was charming enough to make up for that. Her standards had been high, but she believed that at some point, she would find her perfect match. She had always been able to do anything she set her mind to.

"What number was he?"

After a very long pause, Isolde muttered, "Twenty-one."

She had been dumped twenty-one times. If you included the ones she'd broken up with, that number was even higher.

"I see."

Isolde was in her living room at home, sitting across from her older brother. The house was adjoined to the training hall. Isolde's brother, Tantris Cluel, was an Advanced-tier Water God Style swordsman. He was the eldest son of the Cluel family, but compared to his little sister, he was only a minor talent. Despite his grueling efforts, he didn't have what it took to get any higher than the advanced tier. He was an honest man, however. He had even rejected his grandmother Reida when she offered, "How about I make you a Water Saint, eh?" by saying, "I have no need for a title I do not deserve."

When Reida was still alive, she had entrusted him with the management of the training hall—and with Isolde's future.

"Perhaps your standards are too high?"

"I don't think so."

"You're talented and important. You are in a position to choose a suitable match, but if you're too picky, you'll run out of options."

"I know that." Her older brother was a humbling presence in her life. They had lost both their parents while they were still young. Happily, they had their grandmother, the Water God, so they weren't destitute, but their grandmother had been too busy to closely watch children. It was Tantris who had filled the role of Isolde's parent back then, supporting and raising her.

In the training hall, ability was everything. By the time she was ten, Isolde had already outstripped her brother. Even so, she deferred to shared history.

"You don't need to consider the honor of the Cluel family. A harsh destiny will surely await you as Water God. Forget about looks or titles—find a confidant."

Isolde was silent. Tantris was already married and a father. Isolde had met his family, of course, but she did not have a particularly favorable opinion of his wife. She was the daughter of an Asuran noble family. The marriage had been orchestrated solely to foster ties with Water God Reida. She obviously looked down on Tantris, and she had a low opinion of sword fighters. In fact, she hadn't visited the training hall even once. Though they had had a child together, she and Tantris were practically separated. It was because Isolde didn't want to end up in that sort of marriage that she was being cautious in her choice of husband.

Of course, she was not so careful as to not be bowled over by a pretty face. All the same, she had set a standard that they had to be at least an Intermediate-tier sword fighter. She didn't think she was hung up on titles.

Her opportunities to guard Ariel had increased since she became a sword instructor, and as a result, the people she talked to all had titles as well. She would have been fine with a poor noble, a commoner, or even an adventurer if it came to that. They just had to have *something* to make up for it.

"I don't mean to be picky," she said at last.

"Then why not leave the choice to me?"

"No, I'll at least find my own husband myself."

Isolde would not budge. It didn't help that Tantris only introduced her to ugly men. While she insisted she wasn't being picky, she wouldn't compromise on that point. Marriage with them was all but impossible.

"I see..." Tantris wouldn't openly criticize her. This would not be the first time that the Water God went without a partner. The continuation of the Cluel bloodline was being taken care of by him. He did wish to see his little sister happy, and as she wanted a husband, he wanted to support her. That being said, if she didn't desire his help, then Tantris wasn't going to force it. He might not have talent, but he still knew the way of the Water God Style.

"By the way, Isolde, weren't you summoned by Her Majesty today?"

"Yes," Isolde replied after a pause.

"You're not going to be late, are you?"

"I have time."

"It would be terrible for you to keep Her Majesty waiting. Let's leave things here for today."

"Very well. I'll be back later, Brother." Isolde bowed, then returned to her room. She would make herself presentable before setting off for the palace.

When she was gone, Tantris let out a sigh. *A marriage before she takes the Water God's name is looking impossible,* he thought as he made his way to the training hall to instruct his students.

Isolde walked through the Silver Palace of Asura. Her silver breastplate, upon which was emblazoned a crest of a shield-bearing battle maiden, clinked with each step. Her blue and white cloak billowed behind her, and her boots clicked as she strode along. The soldiers on patrol who saw her pass stood to attention, planting their spears on the ground. Their eyes were full of longing. Everyone in the palace knew the name of Water Emperor Isolde, and her noble figure was the object of many a soldier's admiration. Few would dream her thoughts were occupied with things like *I don't want to be a spinster* and *I wonder if there are any good guys around...*

"Why, if it isn't Miss Isolde. Where are you off to?" A man stood before her, blocking her path. Weedy and short with thinning hair, he made for a pathetic figure. He was perhaps in his early forties, a human, and had the look of someone Rudeus might have called the office deadweight. He didn't look anything like a warrior or a swordsman, but he wore a silver breastplate very like Isolde's own, though it bore a different design. His depicted a praying maiden in a mural crown.

"Lord Ifrit. I hope I find you well?"

"Yes, quite well. We are the same rank, so you needn't kneel..."

Sylvester Ifrit was one of the Seven Knights of Asura, known as the Royal Fortress. With a name so ill-befitting his face, he held the highest authority in the guards of the Silver Palace. Isolde was a mere knight. This made her a noble, albeit a lowly one. Sylvester stood at the top of all the knights and soldiers in the palace and was a mid-ranking noble to boot. By custom, Isolde ought to have moved to one side of the corridor, knelt, and stayed that way with her head bowed until he had gone by.

"My lord..."

"We are both Her Majesty's knights," he said, his voice suddenly sharp. Isolde snapped upright.

"Very good," Sylvester said. "It is not the nation we serve, but Her Majesty. The queen is the only one you ought to kneel to." His aura was so formidable that Isolde only nodded.

Sylvester was a small man. He was prone to illness, and he wasn't robust. He wasn't much of a swordsman, nor was he especially good at magic. Yet he had graduated second in his class from the Royal Knights' Academy. He was a master of finding talent and training it up. This was a man who truly understood the importance of putting the right people in the right jobs, and it was because of this single talent that Ariel summoned him back to the capital from the backwater corner of the kingdom and made him her knight.

"Where are you off to anyway, Miss Isolde?"

"Her Majesty summoned me."

"Her Majesty, you say? Well, then, I won't hold you up."

"Don't you need something from me?"

"Oh, it's nothing all that important. My boy said he wanted me to introduce him to you, so if you'll forgive me for indulging my foolish son, I merely wished to ask if you'd meet him, should you have time to spare."

Isolde would have liked to bite. She was intrigued by the talk of a foolish son, but her liege had summoned her.

"Thank you for telling me. Let us speak more about it when you have time," she said with composure, then hurried on her way.

As she made her way deeper into the palace, she passed fewer and fewer people. There were fewer soldiers in plain armor and more knights in expensive armor. These knights were only low-ranking nobles, but they too had sworn their loyalty to Ariel. There was next to no chance they would betray her. In the innermost palace, there were fewer people still. Here there were neither soldiers nor knights, only empty corridors. Occasionally, she passed an unusually sharp-eyed maid—in truth, bodyguards—but no one else. These were Ariel's people, loyal to the bone. Then there were the Royal Chambers, where Ariel resided.

In front of the extravagant door stood a giant of a man clad in golden armor and holding an enormous battle axe. Here was the mightiest gatekeeper in Asura. The chances of him betraying Ariel were non-existent. As well as being in the Golden Knights, he was one of the Seven Knights of Asura: Dohga, the Royal Gatekeeper. He wore a golden helmet in the shape of an upside-down bucket, which bore the design of a battle maiden standing in front of a gate.

"I am Isolde Cluel, here to see Her Majesty."

"Mm." When she said her name, Dohga slowly stirred to life. His movements appeared sluggish, but Isolde knew his guard never dropped for a moment. In a crisis, he could swing that battle axe with terrifying speed, and she suspected that if he fought in earnest, she would be unable to get past him.

"Hm?" Dohga had held a hand out to her. Isolde stared at it, her eyebrows twitching. He had a homely face—not coarse, but not to Isolde's taste. She was a little repulsed at the idea of allowing him to touch her.

"A body search? Go ahead."

These were the queen's rooms. It was to be expected—no one could be permitted to bring a weapon into the monarch's private chambers, knight or not.

Dohga was known for his caution. Even one of the kingdom's ministers would not be permitted to bring in so much as a little wooden spoon after Dohga's careful inspection. Isolde wondered if he would touch her breasts but decided to endure it.

"Mm."

Dohga did not touch Isolde. His hand reached out toward...her hair. And in that hand, he held something.

Isolde looked questioningly at it. Between his fingers, he held a single petal.

"Was stuck."

"Huh?"

"Isolde...you're pretty. Can't leave...thing like this on you." Behind his helmet, Dohga smiled warmly. Isolde stared blankly at him, letting the tension in her body drain away.

"Oh, my weapon." Suddenly remembering, she took her sword from its belt and held it out to Dohga. Dohga did not take it.

"Isolde...you are Queen Ariel's knight. Need weapon. To protect her."

Isolde was silent. He hadn't done a body search, nor had he taken her weapon. As Ariel's knight, she had won this man's trust—this man who numbered among the most able individuals in Asura. When she realized this, her heart began to beat a little faster.

But no way, not with that face... She gave her head a shake, then took a deep breath.

"Isolde Cluel requesting leave to enter."

"Please, come in."

Isolde waited until she heard Ariel's reply, then went into the room.

The Seven Knights of Asura were led by Luke Notos Greyrat, the Royal Dagger, who had sworn absolute loyalty to Ariel. The Seven Knights held a special position among the knights and were allowed a degree of independence. Isolde was one of them. She was the Royal Shield—a fitting title for a Water God Style swordswoman who would protect the queen. Isolde, Sylvester, and Dohga were the Three Knights of the Left, who were responsible for guarding Ariel. The Seven Knights of Asura had sworn absolute loyalty to Ariel—at least, in theory. Isolde didn't know how they were selected. They were supposed to be loyal to Ariel, but most of them had come from elsewhere and had no ties to the kingdom. It was likely that each had something that guaranteed they would never betray Ariel.

But not Isolde. She knew in her heart she could turn traitor. She knew it because during Ariel's battle to seize the throne, her grandmother, the last Water God, was slain in battle by Ariel's ally, Dragon God Orsted.

Isolde was a swordswoman; she understood this was a reality of war. In death, her grandmother had passed the role of Water God on to her. If she turned on Ariel, Water God Style might be driven from the Asura Kingdom, so she had never thought of betraying Ariel. It was simply a practical consideration.

Despite this, nobody who knew her history could ever fully trust her. No one could see inside her heart. She might have been nurturing a grudge over the death of her grandmother in secret, biding her time until she could make an attempt on Ariel's life. Or she might target the killer, Dragon God Orsted. Many aristocrats and knights had been murdered when Ariel took the throne and still harbored resentment over it. They swore their loyalty to Ariel with blithe expressions and bided their time.

Isolde could easily have been seen to hold such intentions, given her position. She had taken the knights' oath and sworn loyalty to Ariel. She hadn't been charmed by Ariel nor was she a patriot—she had done it to defend her position and her pride as a Water God Style practitioner. At present, Ariel's trust in her protected her, but if that changed, Isolde wouldn't stay loyal under any conditions whatsoever. This wasn't a plan, just an understanding of what she was capable of. And yet she had been selected as one of the Seven Knights. It was an odd choice. There had to be a reason for it.

"Isolde. Would you be open to me arranging a few meetings with potential marriage partners?"

When Ariel made this suggestion to her in the royal chambers, Isolde was extremely wary.

"Why involve yourself, Your Majesty?"

"Because you are going to be Water God. It will benefit me as well if you were to settle down with someone. The candidates I have in mind are all related to me by blood, and while many of them have some slightly *difficult* proclivities... Well, one of them may be to your liking."

"Related to Your Majesty... You mean royalty?!"

"Yes, that is how that works."

Potential marriage partners who were *royalty*. Isolde couldn't help it; her heart began pounding. She was such an easy mark.

"But when I become Water God, they'll have to forsake their family name. Won't that be unfavorable for someone from the royal family?"

"Even without their name, the blood tie will remain. There is no requirement that they cut *all* ties with their family, is there?"

"Well, no."

"Then you need not worry. They understand. I have promised them that even if they marry you, the royal family will continue our unwavering support. You need only meet them and choose the one you like best."

This had to be a scheme to win her over, Isolde thought. The terms were too good. Even if they were from some minor branch, royalty related to Ariel by blood were genuine princes. Their chances of becoming king might be microscopic, but still. Also, everyone in Ariel's family was good-looking and sophisticated.

"Well? I think it's an appealing proposition."

"It is!" Isolde replied with enthusiasm. She had no reason to refuse. If she had been a worldly Asuran noble, she might have considered what Ariel left unsaid and refused. Alas, Isolde was only a swordswoman—and a maiden looking for a husband to boot. She didn't read much into it.

"Very good. Please let Luke or Sylvester know when you are free. I will take care of the rest."

"Yes, ma'am. Thank you, ma'am."

"Yes, yes. You may go now."

Isolde left Ariel's chambers as though in a dream. *Marriage meetings with royalty...* Maybe it was her imagination, but she barely felt the floor beneath her. Her heart pounded. She would go to Sylvester immediately and tell him her days off. As she was thinking, she realized her throat was parched. Maybe she had been a little nervous over being summoned unexpectedly.

"I'm thirsty."

"Mm."

Just as she murmured to herself, someone called out from behind her. Isolde dropped into a lower stance, spun around, and came face-to-face with Dohga. He was holding a tiny cup entirely out of proportion with his massive body.

"Here. It's cold."

Isolde took it slowly. "Thank you." For a moment, she wondered if it was poisoned, but then she tipped the contents into her mouth and gulped it down. Feeling the water permeating deep inside her, Isolde realized she was more nervous and much more tired than she'd thought.

"Whew," she breathed.

"Isolde...good work." He smiled. Even through the slit in his helmet, she could tell he had no hint of an ulterior motive.

He was attentive. The thought came naturally to her: this was a man whom she'd let watch her back. Too bad his face wasn't to her taste.

"Same to you, Dohga," she said. "Keep up the good work with your guard duties."

"Mm!"

Well, it was what it was. Imagining the days of meeting with prospective marriage partners who awaited her with sharp-toothed grins, Isolde went on her way.

CHAPTER 2

Dohga the Gatekeeper

IN THE KINGDOM of Asura, there were seven warriors known as the Seven Knights of Asura. They swore absolute loyalty to Ariel Anemoi Asura. Their leader was Knight Banneret Luke Notos Greyrat—the Royal Dagger.

The Three Knights of the Right presided over offense. They were Sandor von Grandeur, the Royal Greatsword; Oswald Euros Greyrat, the Royal Halberd; and Ghislaine Dedoldia, the Royal Guard Dog.

The Three Knights of the Left presided over defense. They were Dohga, the Royal Gatekeeper; Sylvester Ifrit, the Royal Fortress; and Isolde Cluel, the Royal Shield.

Of these seven, the backgrounds and origins of some were widely known, but half of them had been scouted especially by Ariel and Luke. They were a motley bunch, comprising commoners, nobles of all ranks, and a half-human-half-immortal demon. What they all shared was their unswerving loyalty to Ariel. While Isolde suffers for her misunderstanding of what Ariel meant by "slight" when she spoke of "difficult proclivities," let us turn to the story of another of these knights.

He was born in a little village in the Donati Region of Asura. A little slow at times, the other children looked down on him. But he was a healthy child, sturdily built, and never got sick. His father was one of the few soldiers who protected the village and was seldom home. He hardly ever had a day off, and it wasn't unusual for him to be out all night. When the boy was five, his little sister was born. She was a sweet girl, just like their mother. But their mother's recovery after the birth went poorly, and she died.

The boy cried. He hadn't so much as whimpered when his friends punched him or when a mosquito stung him, but now he wailed.

As he wept, his father told him, "It's all right to cry now. But when you're done, you are to protect your sister for me."

The boy looked up at his father, who was holding his little sister, and nodded over and over again. From that day on, the boy stopped crying. He faithfully did as his father had told him—he would protect his little sister.

He decided that the way to do this was to guard the entrance to the house. He took the axe they used for firewood in hand and stood outside the door all day long. It was only when his sister started crying that he ran back inside to tend to her.

His friends laughed at him when they saw him. "What're you doing? Go watch her inside."

The adults of the village said, "Why don't we take her and watch her? We have lots of children already. Another one won't be any trouble."

But the boy dug in his heels and refused to listen. He learned how to look after a nursing infant, and he would not leave the care of his sister to anyone else.

During this time, something unusual happened in the village. One night, all the hapless animals inside one of the barns were devoured. From the footprints, the villagers guessed it was a wolf. The soldiers ran around the village telling the villagers they must bolt their doors and not open them under any circumstances.

The next day, the animal struck a house. Somehow, the wolf had slipped inside under cover of darkness and snapped a child's neck in its jaws, killing them instantly, before escaping through a window. When the family woke up in the morning, none of them knew what had happened. They followed the trail of blood until, just outside the village, they found the baby's clothing lying in a pool of blood. It drove them half-mad.

As more incidents followed, the soldiers realized that their guess had been wrong. The creature stalking the village was not a wolf—it was a monster. It was small, no bigger than an ordinary wolf, but a vicious monster nonetheless.

They were right: it had the head of a wolf and the hind legs of a wolf, but monkey arms sprouted from its shoulders. It could walk on two legs when it chose, and it climbed trees. Though it was only the size of a large dog, its head was too large for its body. It was a clever mutant that had learned the taste of human flesh.

As though it relished the villagers' terror, it lurked in another household's wheatfield for a day to select its next target. It chose its next house because the adult did not come home at night. The father went hunting for the monster elsewhere, leaving his two children helpless. Licking its chops, the monster used its monkey arms to climb up on the roof, then slipped down the chimney.

The next day dawned. When his nighttime patrol was over, the boy's father went back to his house. The first thing that met his eyes was a pool of blood.

"No," he gasped. His face pale, he looked around the house and immediately saw the mangled corpse on the floor. It was the monster, its head split in two. Standing between it and his daughter, who was sleeping peacefully in her bed, was his son. The boy clutched the firewood axe with his legs planted firmly apart, a ferocious look on his face. It had been a desperate battle. The boy was covered in blood, and his arm was broken, but the children were alive. The monster had been small, yes, but it was still the size of a wolf—in other words, twice the boy's size. The child had beaten the monster to death with a blunt firewood axe to protect his sister.

For the boy, who would later become North Emperor Dohga, this was his first battle.

Dohga was a gatekeeper all his life.

When he was ten, he guarded the gate to the village. Just before the displacement incident, there was a great rampage of monsters. They sprang up out of all the forests throughout the kingdom and many villages were swept up in the destruction. Some were even swallowed in the stampede.

Dohga's village was attacked as well, but Dohga took up his woodcutter's axe with undaunted valor, and he drove them off. It was said that he slew anywhere between fifty and a hundred of them. However, despite the great mound of monster corpses Dohga created, his father was killed in the fighting. Dohga stood before his father's lifeless body, stunned. A knight who saw him fight recommended that Dohga go join the guard of the kingdom's capital. Dohga was reluctant, saying he was protecting his little sister.

This was what the knight told him: "Listen well, boy. We leave our families to ride out to all corners of the kingdom, protecting its villages. When the kingdom is safe, our families can live in peace. Protecting the kingdom means protecting your family as well."

Dohga was not bright, and at the time, he did not understand what the knight was saying. In the end, it was money that convinced him. With his father dead, he needed a way to make ends meet. He was told that if he went to the capital, he could earn enough for him and his sister to live on, so that decided that. Dohga became a soldier of the royal capital.

He was posted to a little gate that separated the slums from the lower-class citizens' district. The gate existed as a bottleneck for when the people of the slums grew unruly and stormed the lower-class district. It was forbidden for any to pass at night, but otherwise, it had no special importance. It was a suitable post for an uneducated boy from the countryside.

The room he and his sister were given to live in was small but serviceable. From there, he went to work at the barracks. He stood at the gate from morning to night, and sometimes even the whole night that followed.

Although slow, Dohga was also strangely endearing. At first, some of the other soldiers resented that, at barely ten, he was serving with them. But his innocent nature and steadfast dedication to his sister melted the hearts of his comrades, and before his first year was up, they had recognized him as one of their own.

He began his second year.

One night, a woman came running to Dohga's gate. She threw herself on him, begging for his help. When Dohga hesitated, a group of hard-faced men appeared and yelled at him, "Hand over the girl!"

Dohga was confused. He didn't know what to do. If only Hans, who was supposed to be on duty with Dohga, hadn't been napping, he might have decided for them.

When the woman saw Dohga's confusion, she tried to dash away through the gate. Dohga immediately grabbed her collar and pulled her back. He had been told that no one was to pass the gate at night.

In that moment, the men, sensing that the woman was going to get away, attacked. Dohga swung his battle axe—a farewell gift from the village smith when he had become a soldier. He killed all the men. At the sight of Dohga standing there, drenched in blood, the woman wet herself, then sunk down on all fours.

Hans came running, drawn by the noise. He stopped short at the sight of the carnage at the gate. This, he thought, was going to be bad. Dohga had committed an act of indiscriminate murder. Hans had been asleep; the blame would fall on him, too. His face gray, he went to check the corpses, then he realized he knew these faces. It was the gang of thieves who had been running wild through the lower-class district. This lot had been giving the guard a lot of trouble because the knights wouldn't bother with this lowly district.

And Dohga had wiped them all out single-handedly.

Dohga was promoted. He went from being the soldier who guarded the gate between the lower-class district and the slum to the soldier who guarded the gate between the middle-class district and the lower-class district. For some reason, Hans went with him.

Dohga stayed at that gate for some time. Some days it rained, some days a gale blew through, but he stood watch through it all. Even after he came of age, he stuck to it. He was slow, so Hans helped him.

Along the way, Hans came to understand Dohga better than anyone. Dohga's sister grew up into a beautiful young woman, and she and Hans were married. Perhaps Hans had been eyeing his sister all along, but that didn't matter to Dohga—he knew that while Hans might nap on the job, he wasn't a bad sort. He swore to Saint Millis in front of Dohga that he would make his sister happy.

But then Dohga found himself alone. With his sister married, he'd fulfilled his father's instructions through to the end. He no longer needed to guard any gate.

Yet Dohga stayed at his post.

Some days it rained, some days a gale blew through, but he guarded the gate.

On one such day, the city was rocked by a great shock: Ariel Anemoi Asura had announced her coronation. A coronation ceremony was a celebration that lasted for days. The soldiers would get a pay raise for the duration as well as free food. Dohga's comrades were delighted; Hans even did a little dance.

This also meant that they would have to do more work.

Security needed to be tightened not only in the middle-class district, but throughout the entire city. Temporary guards were recruited from among the city folk, while Dohga and the others who were already soldiers were assigned to guard more important locations. Dohga and Hans did their job with gusto, thinking they would buy Dohga's little sister something nice with their extra wages.

One day, around halfway through the coronation, Dohga found himself guarding the servants' entrance to the palace. Few people passed there, but every now and then, a servant with a pass would come through. Hans was not with him. Dohga guarded this gate together with several other soldiers.

A man came along. He wore shabby old armor and carried a long staff.

"I couldn't convince you to let me pass, could I? I seek an audience with Queen Ariel."

Of course the guard on the gate turned him away. "None may pass this gate without permission! Produce your pass!"

"I do not have a pass. I would like to beg an audience with the queen."

"No pass, no passage. Away with you!"

"I have no choice, then. I'm glad I came to this gate. I thought I might have to cast a pall on Her Majesty's glorious occasion," the man said. He tried to force his way through the gate. His staff moved like magic. In an instant, the other gatekeepers were knocked to the ground.

But not Dohga. No matter how many times the man drove the butt of his staff into Dohga's vital spots, he remained standing. Dohga swung his axe at the man but couldn't touch him. Dohga had never before missed a target. He went on attacking doggedly.

The man was delighted. "Marvelous! I didn't think to find a man like you hidden away in a place like this. All right. Out of respect for your strength, I will give up on getting through this gate. I beg your pardon. As a token of my apology, how about becoming my apprentice? You've got talent!"

Dohga had no idea what the man was talking about, but the man seemed to have given up on getting through the gate. But the moment he relaxed, he passed out. He didn't even drop; he was out cold and still standing. When he woke with a start, the man was still there. He was holding Dohga's axe and appeared to be guarding the gate—except that he was surrounded by a throng of soldiers.

"Good morning, kid! I've been guarding the gate for you!"

That was how Dohga met Sandor—otherwise known as Alex Rybak, North God Kalman II.

The day that Dohga became Sandor's apprentice, he went home and half-collapsed into bed. There had been a healing magician among the soldiers who had come running, so none of the damage was permanent. His battle with North God Kalman had drained every drop of his bottomless reserves of strength. For the first time in his life, he fell asleep out of exhaustion. He slept for two days, then woke up. At his bedside was his sister, tear streaks on her face, and Hans, who looked relieved. Also, there was Sandor, looking inappropriately cheerful.

"Good morning, apprentice! Come with me." In a terrific display of strength, Sandor pulled Dohga to his feet, then got him into his armor and made to lead him off somewhere. Dohga, not understanding, looked to Hans for help.

"Sorry, Dohga. I don't really know what's going on either, but I think you're being honored. So look, go along with him for now, eh? You do your best, and don't be rude."

"Yes," his sister added. "Brother, I... Please do your best."

Dohga, not following Hans's train of thought at all, looked around in confusion, but he couldn't fight Sandor's strength. And so, they set off for the gate he had guarded the other day. When they arrived, Sandor pulled out a pass with a flourish to let them through. Just like that, they were inside the palace. Dohga followed behind Sandor, amazed by his first glimpse of the glittering halls. Before he knew it, there was a pretty woman with blonde hair in front of him.

"This is the boy?"

"Yes, Your Majesty!"

"I wish to speak to him a little."

Sandor gave Dohga a shove in the back, so that he was standing directly in front of the woman. She was divinely beautiful.

"I am Ariel Anemoi Asura. And you are?"

Dohga did not know that name. Though he was a city soldier, he was unaware of the queen. Naturally, he had never seen her either. Before he knew it, Dohga found himself kneeling. For some reason he felt like he ought to.

"I-I'm...Dohga."

"Why did you become a soldier?"

"D-Dad...said protect...little sister, so..."

Dohga struggled with speaking. He had never been eloquent enough to recount his life to anyone, but Ariel readily accepted what he said.

"To protect your sister? Very admirable."

"B-but...now Hans protects...my sister, I mean, they're together now...um..."

At a glance from Ariel, the knight beside him supplied, "His younger sister married a soldier named Hans." Dohga didn't know this, but the knight was Luke.

"So I...don't really have to protect...her anymore..."

Ariel smiled at Dohga's slightly dejected expression. "You are wrong, Dohga," she said.

"Huh?"

"You do still have to protect her."

"Wh-what do you...mean?"

"Hans is your younger brother now. That means that you have to protect both of them. You have to do twice the work."

That was a shock to Dohga. He hadn't thought about it like that. She was right, though. Hans, who said he would protect Dohga's sister, *had* started to call him brother. Dohga was his older brother. He had to protect his little sister, so obviously, he had to protect his little brother too.

"O-oh. I...need to protect them more?"

"That's right. If you keep doing what you've always done, you might not be able to protect either of them."

"Huh?! Wh-why?"

"You are strong, but your reach is short. It may be that the two of them will run into danger somewhere you cannot help them."

Dohga looked at the palms of his hands. He remembered how his father had died. He had been so close, and yet a monster had killed him when Dohga wasn't looking.

"Th-then...what should I...do?"

"Protect me."

"Huh?"

"I serve the kingdom. I make it better. By protecting me, you will be protecting the kingdom, and by protecting the kingdom, you will be protecting your brother and sister."

Dohga didn't understand. What did protecting this woman in front of him have to do with protecting Hans and his sister? He was completely lost. But Ariel was serious. He remembered that someone else had told him something similar—the knight who had given him a letter of recommendation to join the city guard.

Listen well, boy. We leave our families to ride out to all corners of the kingdom, protecting its villages. When the kingdom is safe, our families can live in peace. Protecting the kingdom means protecting your family as well.

At the time, he hadn't known what he was being told. It was money that had spurred him into action. Now, he felt like he understood. After all, even when he was protecting a totally different place, his sister and Hans lived happily.

"Dohga. Will you swear loyalty to me? Will you protect me and, by extension, the kingdom?"

"Yes, Your Majesty."

"Very well, Dohga, I name you a knight." On that day, Dohga became one of the Seven Knights of Asura.

Since then, Dohga had guarded the final gate—the door to the royal chambers. Sometimes, on Ariel's orders, he went other places. For a few hours each day, he practiced under Sandor's tutelage a short distance from Ariel's chambers.

On the one day each month he had leave, he went to eat dinner with his sister and Hans. When Dohga wasn't there, someone else guarded the royal chambers in his place. Usually, it was Isolde Cluel, the Royal Shield, but that was not the case in the beginning.

After being made a knight and given his shining gold armor, he had stubbornly refused to budge from in front of *his* gate. Now that he had made up his mind to protect it, he could not hand it off to anyone who'd do the job half-heartedly. For his first month, he would not surrender his post to anyone except Sandor. If Ariel had not ordered him to rest, he would have stayed on guard for days without food or drink or sleep. He performed body searches on everyone who approached the royal chambers without distinguishing between men and women. He would confiscate even the tiniest fork.

It was around this time that a new member joined the Seven Knights of Asura—Isolde Cluel, the Royal Shield. She had her job as sword instructor, but back then, before Ghislaine joined them, she was the only woman among the Seven Knights. It was decided that she was the ideal choice for the queen's personal protection.

One day, it was decided that Sandor would travel around the Asura Kingdom to put together the Golden Knights. Without Sandor, there was no one who could fill in for Dohga. If he stood there for a full month, he would collapse. So Sandor set up a match between him and Isolde.

At that time, Sandor had Dohga introduce himself as "North King." He had only just begun his training, but he was extremely skilled. Even so, Isolde wiped the floor with him. She moved like the wind, turning aside his blows from his battle axe, then hammering him with one counterattack after another until she brought him down. If they had been using real blades and fighting to kill, Isolde would have slain Dohga in an instant.

Dohga had an inexhaustible supply of strength, but he lost without laying so much as a finger on her. This woman, slender as a flower, had turned aside the blows of an axe broader than she was, then stung like a delicate thorn. After taking strike after strike, Dohga accepted that this was a person worthy of guarding the door in his stead.

He also understood something: the woman was a delicate and beautiful flower, untouchable to the likes of him. Dohga was in love.

"You seem down lately..."

Dohga was at dinner with his sister and her husband. The food on the table was simple, but there was enough of it to fill even Dohga's giant belly. On the other side of the table sat his sister and Hans, and beside Hans, their lovely daughter.

Dohga, a brimming tankard of wine in one hand, looked blankly at Hans.

"Are you not feeling well?"

"Wh-why?" Dohga said as he tried to mask his inner turmoil.

Hans pointed at the food. "You've barely eaten."

Dohga looked. It was true; he'd hardly made a dent in the food. He loved his sister's cooking. Usually, Dohga gulped down his food in silence, happily stuffing his cheeks until he'd polished everything off. The same went for wine, which was his favorite. It was only drunk on celebratory occasions, but when they had it, he drank like a fish. Hans kept an entire barrel on hand for those occasions. Yet for some reason, Dohga had only eaten half his food, and he only sipped at his wine. Something was wrong.

"If you don't feel well, you get one of the palace healing magicians to look at you, all right? They'd do that for you, what with you being a knight now, yeah? Though I have to say, you look healthy enough."

Dohga tilted his head, face blank. He didn't realize there was anything unusual about himself.

"If you're worn out, why not ask for a few more days off? I know you're a hard worker and you've got an honorable job in guarding Her Majesty. If you push yourself too hard and collapse, then where will you be? Not that I could imagine you collapsing."

"Mm." Dohga nodded and started to eat. Something was definitely off. The food tasted how it always did—delicious. It just felt wrong as he swallowed it. Usually, it was more munching and gulping and yelling, "Bring out the next dish!"

Not today.

Every time he swallowed, his stomach rejected it. It was like the feeling of being full, but more unpleasant. The wine was strange too—it was tasteless. This had never happened to him before. Perhaps he really was sick or, like Hans said, worn out.

"Hey now, what's the story? Tell us." When Dohga stayed silent, Hans pressed further. "Brother... Dohga. Ever since we were guards down in the lower city, you've always had my back. If you can't tell me your troubles, I won't be able to show my face anywhere—not even to Saint Millis."

"Mm. I don't...know either."

"Something must've happened recently at the palace. Anything. Just try to talk," Hans said with a serious look.

Dohga looked up. Then, just as Hans had said, he went through his memories and, bit by bit, began to talk them through. There was the cat that had gotten lost inside while he was watching the final gate. He had given it some of his lunch, and it had started coming by a lot, which made him happy. How when he was walking through the town in his armor, a young soldier flagged him down to say, "I respect you," which had made him happy. Isolde had come by while he was guarding the final gate, then thanked him when he took a flower petal from her hair and gave it to her, which had made him happy. When Sandor had taught him a new technique, he'd said, "You really have talent," which had made him happy. While he was walking around the hospital, a guard shared a rumor with him that "Isolde might get married." That didn't make him happy. How at a party for the guards, Isolde had come in a dress and been the most beautiful woman he'd ever seen, which had made him happy. He had seen her dancing with men he didn't know, which hadn't made him happy. How the noble girls had been spreading groundless rumors about Isolde, which had made him unhappy. How he had seen Isolde walking together with a handsome man, which had hurt his heart. How Isolde—

"That's enough. I understand. I understand perfectly," Hans said, cutting Dohga off. He had the general idea now. "You're in love with this Isolde, eh?"

Dohga's cheeks burned. He didn't know how Hans had worked it out from what he'd said, but he'd hit the nail on the head.

"You heard that Isolde's going to get married, then you saw things that seemed to give weight to it, and it gave you a shock."

After a long pause, Dohga mumbled, "Mm." The gloom hanging over him was palpable.

Hans was right. His big brother, who he'd thought was oblivious to matters of the heart, was in love.

A memory came back to Hans of his own first love. She was the daughter of the greengrocer next door to his family home. Though they were five years apart in age, they were childhood friends, and she had taken care of him ever since he was small. She was kind, reliable, and pretty, and he fell in love with her at only five years old. He'd dreamed of marrying her. When he was older, he thought, he would enlist as a soldier. Once he had a stable income, he would ask for her hand in marriage.

In the summer of his twelfth year, she married the butcher's son and took up his family trade. Hans knew her husband, who had already been old in his earliest memories. He would have been about five years older than her. Come to think of it, that meant he couldn't have been that old.

At first, Hans was in denial. The man was well built, but he definitely wasn't handsome. Hans was sure that she hadn't really wanted to get married, and that one day, he would reclaim her. But a year later, when he saw her happily snuggled up in her husband's arms, her belly huge, it finally hit him. He had cried into his pillow. Maybe if he'd told her how he felt earlier, it would all have been different.

Not that he was unhappy now, of course. If he had married the greengrocer's daughter, he couldn't have married Dohga's little sister. She wasn't like Dohga at all—she was slight and sweet and steadfast. The fruit of their love was now shoveling down food in Dohga's place. She was a robust child, and bright—not like Hans. Most of all, she was cute as a button. Hans was confident there could be no one as happy as him, but it had come on the tail of bitter heartbreak.

Thanks to that experience, he sprang into action as soon as he realized how he felt about Dohga's sister. She might have thought him a little frivolous at first, but Hans had always been a gentleman with her. He worked harder than ever at his job as gatekeeper. Since he told her that he loved her, he hadn't slept with a prostitute once. As a result, he had won out over no small number of rivals to claim the happiness he had now.

That was why Hans said, "Ask Isolde to marry you right away."

Dohga looked up blankly.

"You don't have to get hitched immediately. You could just do a betrothal. You just need to tell her how you feel."

Dohga didn't say anything.

"If you stand by for much longer, you'll regret it."

"But..."

"Don't worry about whether you're a good match for each other. You're one of Asura's Golden Knights. We in the guards are proud of you, and we look up to you. Hold your head high and put yourself out there."

Dohga thought a little. He didn't know what made people compatible, but he knew a little about looks. Isolde was too beautiful to be a good match for him.

"You don't need to expect anything. Tell her how you feel and get your heart broken. At this rate, you won't be able to wish her well on her wedding day."

At these words, Dohga immediately made up his mind. He was going to tell Isolde how he felt.

CHAPTER 3

Isolde and Dohga

"HOW MANY IS IT NOW?" Isolde had left the training hall and was at home, sitting across from her brother in the living room.

"Twenty-six," she muttered, not looking up. Tantris tried to catch her eye, but Isolde kept hers averted.

"A little bird told me it was you who turned them down."

"Yeah."

"Why?"

Isolde pressed her lips together. "It's just, I don't know... They're all fine men. Good-natured, gentle... But..."

"But?"

"Maybe they're *too* good. It makes their flaws stand out." They were royalty, introduced to her through Ariel.

They were young and pleasant, and their conversations had been lovely. But...they didn't hold back. Maybe Ariel had said something to them, because they even told her about their fetishes.

There was Atole Orpheus Asura, who was good-looking and kind and said he would devote himself to her after they were married.

There was Basil Venti Asura, who was good-looking and strong and had a deep understanding of Water God Style.

There was Carlos Siodos Asura, who was good-looking and elegant and said he could support Water God Style from a financial perspective after they were married.

There was Daniel Lapis Asura, who was good-looking and funny and made her laugh all through their conversation.

There was Elliot Skiron Asura, who was good-looking and sweet and made her instinctively want to protect him.

But they told her *everything*. They told her what they wanted to do to her in bed and outside of it and the little outfits they'd like to see her in. It was more than Isolde, with her limited experience, could keep up with. They seemed more than a little strange in the head; it honestly made her ill. Before she knew it, she'd cut them off.

Isolde had developed a bit of a distrust of men. She knew not all men were as awful as these, but no small number of men out there wanted to do *those* sorts of things. She almost wanted to give up on marriage altogether.

"Flaws? Such as?"

"I can't tell you. Things I can't speak of."

"Ah... Well, they *are* Asuran royalty." Asuran aristocrats were infamous for their perversions. The higher echelons of the nobility were too spoiled for normal tastes.

"That puts you in a tough spot, though. I didn't think you would turn them all down."

"Not all of them... I mean, there are still a few more."

"Be that as it may, it isn't looking promising, is it?" Tantris said.

Whenever she got to choose something herself, Isolde had always had a tendency to be too selective—*I don't like that one, not that one either...* In the meantime, the best options were snatched up by someone else, and she had to take whatever was left. Marriage was no different.

"All right," Tantris said at last. "This is what we'll do." With due consideration of his sister's personality, Tantris made up his mind. "You will marry the next one."

"But I can't just..."

"I am sure he will not meet your standards. You get hung up on their failings because you are in a position to be selective. Once you are married and living together, such flaws may come to seem trivial. You may grow to appreciate him."

Tantris didn't like this sort of strong-arm logic. He thought Isolde needed time to choose, to get to know the other person to their core. But Ariel arranging this made him think that this forceful approach could work out. If Ariel had introduced her to these men, surely she couldn't go too far astray.

He gave her too much credit.

After a long silence, Isolde made up her mind. "All right." It was true, she was being too picky. She'd always been like that and probably would be all her life. That part of her personality was well-suited to Water God Style, and she was on the verge of becoming Water God herself. But when it came to marriage, it was a problem. At this rate, she'd end up spending her whole life alone.

The position of Water God was esteemed. The people who knew her would give her admiration, praise, and commendations. She would smile back at them, talk to them, then when she was feeling good, she would go home to an empty room to eat a meal for one, get ready for bed, and sleep alone.

That sounded so empty.

You didn't become Water God to win praise. Inside, there was another Isolde, separate from the swordswoman. She was always lonely, and that was why she felt empty. She didn't know if a husband and children would comfort the other Isolde, but if she had all the praise in the world, she wanted to come home to someone and say how proud she was of herself.

And then, after she was done boasting, her pervert husband would ask her to do something rotten.

But she had made up her mind.

"So where and when are you meeting the next candidate?"

"Today. I'm told he's coming to get me in a carriage."

"Royalty is coming to...pick you up?"

"Yes."

There were three candidates left. Isolde was unaware of this, but after hearing that she had rejected five suitors out of hand, the rest had gotten serious. They decided the order in which they would meet her through a stringent lottery. They were ready to mount their attacks.

"Huh?" Just then, something caught Isolde's attention. "There's some sort of commotion over in the training hall."

The training hall adjoined the Cluel house, but this place was the headquarters of Water God Style, so it had quiet flooring to match. Usually, you couldn't hear anything from where they were, but Isolde was a Water Emperor. She could hear the violence.

"Could he be here already?"

"It's still too early, but I might have mistaken the time. I'd better go. I can't run the risk of offending royalty."

"That's true. Best hurry." Isolde and Tantris shared a nod, then set off for the training hall.

The hall was in a tumult. The disciples in their training gear stood gathered around a man, heaping angry shouts and taunts at him.

"Master! A challenger has come from a rival school! He showed up out of nowhere and demanded to see you!"

The blood drained from Isolde and Tantris's faces. If their students had subjected a member of the royal family to such treatment, the whole training hall might be torn down. Had he not given his name?

"Stop that!" Isolde shouted. The hall fell silent. "Clear the way! That man is my guest!"

"But... But he's—"

"All of you, on your knees at the edge of the hall!" At Isolde's order, the students scattered like baby spiders and sat down in lines. The students had been trained to do that from way back in her grandmother's time.

But that wasn't important. Right now, she needed to apologize. With the students out of the way, Isolde looked over at the man.

Huh? She found herself looking at an enormous man. He was more than two meters tall, and his shoulders had to be close to a meter across. He was built like a boulder. Isolde knew that boulder.

"Dohga?"

"Mm." He turned around when she called out to him. It *was* him—none other than Dohga, the Royal Gatekeeper, one of the Seven Knights of Asura. He looked out of place, almost shrinking back in fear. But when he saw Isolde, a relieved smile broke over his face.

"I just saved your lives," Isolde told her students. "This man is North Emperor Dohga. If he wanted to, he could take all of you out with one..."

That was as far as she got before she realized what Dohga was wearing. That was a knight's ceremonial uniform. Isolde had never seen him in it before. He only ever wore his golden armor or his gray armor. Ariel never said anything about it. In addition to his unusually tight outfit, he had a bouquet in his hand. In the vastness of Dohga's fist, the bouquet looked small, but it was, in fact, enormous.

"Why are you here? Did something happen to Her Majesty? Is it an emergency?" Isolde asked, furrowing her brow. In response, Dohga moved slowly toward her, then held out the bouquet in his hand.

Could it be?

He was in a formal uniform and holding a bouquet.

Of course she also thought, *It can't be!* But her first thought won out.

"I...Isolde Cluel... I... I love you! Please...m-marry me!"

Could it be that *Dohga* was a member of the Asuran royal family?

She was struck by a thought. Dohga was the only man entrusted with guarding Ariel in her private chambers. Luke was a special case, but even Sandor wasn't allowed to bring a weapon near those rooms. He even stood outside her door in the middle of the night. As far as Isolde knew, he wasn't a eunuch. People said he was safe and harmless, but he was still a man. With his enormous size and the martial skill of a North Emperor, breaking into Ariel's room as she slept would be easy for him. Isolde had always wondered why Ariel had chosen a man like him. If he was Ariel's relative, if they had known each other well since they were children...

She had heard that Dohga had come from a tiny village on the outskirts of the kingdom, but royalty came from everywhere. Just as Ariel had once fled to a faraway land, Dohga might have been in hiding during his childhood.

"Isolde." At Tantris's voice, Isolde emerged from the ocean of her thoughts.

She might have just avoided a nasty situation. Perhaps Dohga was a dark secret of the Asura Kingdom. If she'd been careless, even *she* might have found herself erased.

"What's wrong?" Tantris asked.

She had to face reality. "Nothing..." she said, then looked at Dohga again.

He had just said, "Please marry me." There was no mistaking that. Isolde had once been desperate to hear those words. She couldn't have misheard. Dohga radiated confidence. He had confidently strode in through the front gate, handed her a bouquet, then proposed to her.

Isolde had imagined something more romantic, but in the right light, maybe this *was* romantic. Holding out a bouquet before proposing in front of a crowd of people was on Isolde's list of romantic proposals, though obviously in front of a beautiful fountain or at a fancy party, not in a training hall suffused with the stink of sweat...

No, she'd put that out of mind. That, and many other things too.

"It's perfect timing, isn't it?" Tantris said tentatively. "He's another of the glorious Seven Knights of Asura. You'd make a well-matched pair."

"Yes... But... I don't..." Isolde realized there were eyes on her—the eyes of her students.

"Let's speak in private. Dohga, please follow me."

"Mm."

Isolde turned to go. When she didn't take the bouquet, Dohga looked sad for a moment, but he followed close after.

That was how Dohga was invited into Isolde's home. Now, he sat frozen on the couch, trying to make himself look as small as possible. The bouquet was laid over his knees. Isolde sat directly opposite him, her posture regal. Her face gave nothing away; it seemed almost as if she didn't have a thought in the world. Tantris was nowhere to be seen. He had left the pair in the reception room and gone to make tea.

Isolde examined Dohga's face. Under her inspection, he assumed a serious expression, but the way his cheeks trembled made it clear how nervous he was.

However, Isolde wasn't concerned with that. She was interested in his face. It was a plain, open face. Not her type. She could close her eyes to all sorts of things, but at the end of the day, she didn't like what she didn't like.

Part of her longed for a chance to reconsider the last five proposals. If their specs were otherwise more or less the same, then those five, by virtue of being nice to look at, were more appealing. But the next member of the royal family to show up might be even less appealing than Dohga. All that aside, there was the matter of her agreement with her brother. She had to decide things here.

She let out a breath, then said, "You know, it was a surprise to find out that you're royalty."

Dohga gaped at her. "Me? Not...royalty."

Isolde hesitated. "Huh? So you were adopted in or something like that?" she asked, attempting to obliquely figure out what he was trying to hide.

"I...born in little village. In Donati. Always been gatekeeper. Dad was village soldier..."

All she got from Dohga was the story of how a totally unexceptional soldier had risen in the world. Well, perhaps not unexceptional. Isolde listened, trying to glean something from what he said. When he got to the part about crying when his little sister had gotten married, she was so invested, she felt the tears well up.

"Then I...hear that you, Isolde, get married. Before that, I wanted to at least say how I feel."

Isolde was silent. He wasn't connected to any of this. He wasn't one of the royals Ariel wanted to introduce her to. In that case, Isolde decided, she would refuse him. It was too bad, but she couldn't snub Ariel.

Hm? Why did I think "too bad"?

The answer came at once. Dohga was honest, hardworking, and devoted. Judging from his words, he didn't have any awful bedroom preferences. He was skilled enough to become a North Emperor, and he was one of the Seven Knights of Asura. He had a stable income. He enjoyed drinking, but he wasn't a violent drunk, and he didn't have any extravagant vices. The only thing wrong with him was his face, and it wasn't *that* bad. He just wasn't quite Isolde's type.

"Uh...um...!" In response to Isolde's frown, Dohga, with what looked like a great effort of will, spoke. "Ev... Ever since I first...see you, I think...Isolde is pretty as... these flowers. I... I always love you!" With that, he held the bouquet out to her again.

"Did you? From the first time you saw me?" Isolde's field of view was all flowers. They were a deep blue color. She didn't know their name, but they were beautiful. A little spark ignited in her heart.

"Mm."

If Isolde remembered correctly, her first encounter with Dohga had been a fight. She had fought him over a matter of Ariel's security. He had felt this way all this time? Thinking back, Dohga had been a little soft with Isolde. He had always trusted her. He hadn't confiscated her weapon when she went into Ariel's chambers. The fact that they were both in the Seven Knights of Asura had to be part of it, but perhaps that wasn't the whole story.

As she thought this, Dohga watched on with an earnest face—a face that now seemed about 20 percent more attractive. Not *so* bad. Striking from the right angle, even. Besides, he usually wore a helmet, so you couldn't even see his face most of the time.

"Wait, wait...!" Isolde shook her head. "I'm very sorry, but I will be marrying a member of the royal family introduced to me by Queen Ariel."

If she were to take up with Dohga now, she could end up bringing shame on Ariel. Isolde was a knight. She hadn't sworn absolute loyalty, but she *had* sworn loyalty. She couldn't shame her liege just to suit her whims.

"You are one of Her Majesty's knights," she went on. "You can't go against her wishes either, can you?"

Dohga looked a little troubled, but said, "Mm." Just like Isolde, Dohga, too, was a knight. He was also diligent. Even if he wasn't royalty, it was this that had won him Ariel's trust and allowed him to become her gatekeeper. He would not betray Ariel either.

"You may go home now," Isolde said.

"Mm."

She'd thought he would protest a little, but Dohga stood up at once, then turned away from Isolde. Just like that. He even seemed to be in good spirits. It was as though he'd known he would be turned down from the start and was satisfied just to have said it. Isolde was a little disappointed by this.

She sighed, then looked at the table. One blue petal lay there. The bouquet was gone. He must have taken it home with him.

"I wish I'd at least taken the flowers..." she murmured, picking up the petal.

Isolde refused the next royal suitor who came that day.

The next day, Isolde was at the parade grounds instructing. As she went through the forms, she ruminated on the previous day.

Her royal suitor had been Fraser Caecius Asura. His perversions had been awful, just like the others, though he wasn't a bad person. Compared to Dohga, however, he struck her as insincere. Still, if she had at least deferred her decision rather than refusing him, she could have avoided offending him.

In any case, there were two left. Only two left. She had to judge them both carefully and choose one, she thought. Just then, a messenger came up to her.

"Miss Isolde! Her Majesty urgently wishes to discuss an apology!" From that, Isolde guessed that Ariel was going to tell her off for refusing one suitor after another. She'd take her licks. She owed Ariel an apology.

"Very well," she said, then left the parade ground. She went into the knights' private room at the exit and brushed the dust off herself. She ought to have washed with water, but given it was urgent, she could get away with not doing so. She set off for the royal chambers at a brisk pace.

"Hm?" As she drew near to the innermost reaches of the palace, she felt something was off. It was noisier than usual. Usually, there were no soldiers or knights here, just empty corridors stretching on and on. But she could see agitated soldiers moving about. *Did something happen?* she wondered. No, the queen's summons took priority. Without pausing to ask them any questions, she hurried to the royal chambers.

Isolde frowned. Someone who ought to have been at the door was absent—an enormous man built like a boulder and clad in golden armor, Asura's mightiest gatekeeper never left this palace so long as Ariel was in her chambers—Dohga. He was nowhere to be seen.

As though to make up for his absence, knights stationed at the palace stood in rows around the royal chambers. They all had weapons at their belts. What a fuss! Every one of them was a veteran as well. There were even knights hailing from low- and middle-ranking noble stock who would never usually have been allowed to venture this far in. That would be Sylvester's leadership. He never considered the repercussions of his decisions.

"Lord Ifrit!" Isolde said, spotting a familiar figure. It was chief of the palace guard Sylvester Ifrit, the Royal Fortress.

"Miss Isolde, you arrived quickly."

"What in the world is going on?" she asked. Sylvester grimaced as though he were trying to think of where to start.

A few seconds passed, then he shrugged and said, "Her Majesty wishes to apologize."

He might as well have said *Go in there and ask.* Giving up on getting an explanation here, Isolde knocked on the door.

"Isolde Cluel to see Her Majesty!"

"Please, come in." Ariel sounded the same as ever. In contrast to the uproar, her voice was perfectly serene.

"Excuse me," Isolde said as she opened the door and entered.

A strange scene met her. Ariel sat at her desk. Beside her were Luke, his arms folded and his face exhausted, and her bodyguards, who glared at her with their weapons drawn, ready to fight. Then there was Dohga. Dohga hardly ever left his post, but there he was. He held his golden helmet under one arm and a slightly sad-looking bouquet in his hand.

"Welcome, Isolde. You were quick."

"I was just in the parade grounds... Your Majesty, what is all this?"

"Dohga tells me he means to resign as my knight," Ariel replied casually.

"He what?!" Isolde looked at Dohga. His face was serious. So this wasn't some sort of prank. "He... You mean... Why would he do that?"

"By all means, ask Dohga..." Ariel said, then added, "Dohga, please repeat your reasons."

Dohga's gaze moved to Ariel, then he nodded. "Isolde... said Queen Ariel's knight...can't marry her."

Eh?! With those brief words from Dohga, Isolde guessed why she had been summoned.

"No! I only said, 'You can't go against her wishes either, can you?' Because I didn't want to bring shame on Her—"

"Isolde, be still and let him finish," Ariel said softly. Isolde fell quiet, but inside, she felt anything but peaceful. If the conversation went the wrong way, it might look as though she had incited Dohga to betray Ariel. In fact, judging from the fuss outside, everyone already saw it that way.

"Dohga."

At Ariel's prompting, he started to speak haltingly. "I... think a lot. I...promise Dad to protect my sister. Lady Ariel said protecting the kingdom means protecting my sister. Lady Ariel's queen, so protecting her means protecting the kingdom. But my sister tells me, she says I've protected her enough. She has no troubles, so now I protect who I love. I...love Lady Ariel. I love this...kingdom. But my love for Isolde...more special. So I resign... as Lady Ariel's knight. Then...I protect Isolde." He set his helmet down on the desk with a *clang.* Then he turned and held the bouquet out to Isolde.

Isolde looked at the blue flowers in front of her, their petals slightly wilted. It was the same bouquet from yesterday.

"So that is what Dohga has to say...but what do *you* say, Isolde?"

"Huh?"

Faced with this sudden profession of love, Isolde blinked hard.

"I do not know what terms you have set, but apparently, he chooses you over the Seven Knights of Asura. The moment all women yearn for, hm? What do you say?"

Ariel wasn't going to accuse her of inciting betrayal. On top of that, she was asking Isolde to answer Dohga.

"B-but all the men Your Majesty introduced me to..."

"Oh, them. Never mind them," Ariel said.

Isolde's heart rattled in her chest even harder than it had when she faced down the Fighting God in the Biheiril Kingdom. She felt like she was going to collapse.

"I... I..." All of a sudden, she remembered the legend of the first Water God and the princess who had thrown away everything to be his wife. Based on what he had told her yesterday, Dohga was a man with almost nothing. He had his size, his strength, a few relatives, and his post in the Seven Knights of Asura. That was all.

He had chosen Isolde.

Even if it meant leaving his family and his post. It'd only been a day. He said he had thought a lot, but his decision had been all but immediate. Dohga had told her that he valued her above anything else. He wasn't like the other nobles or the royal suitors Ariel had sent her. None of them would have pursued Isolde to the point of casting aside the greatest of their possessions, just like the princess who married the first Water God. Dohga might be the only person in the world who would love Isolde this much.

What more could she possibly want? Who cared about how he looked?

Before she knew it, Isolde had taken the bouquet, that enormous bunch of blue flowers. They were just a little past their prime. Dohga would still love and keep the flowers, even if they withered. In the end, youth and beauty didn't last.

"I'm yours, if you'll have me," Isolde said.

"Mm!" Dohga beamed at her as applause broke out from around them.

The story of the proposal in the royal chambers was on everyone's lips after that, trickling down to even the lowest ranks of soldiers. Dohga's former comrades cried with joy, and all of Isolde's admirers cried into their pillows. Dohga resigned from the Seven Knights of Asura to become Isolde's husband. Instead of Dohga of the Seven Knights, he was now Dohga the househusband... or that was the plan.

"You say you mean to resign as a knight. Isolde is a knight of this kingdom too. She is very strong, but if I died and the kingdom became unstable, she could be murdered. You will protect her, of course, but even then... Of course, that won't happen so long as I do not die. What say you, Dohga? While you protect Isolde, could you protect me as well?"

Taken in by Ariel's honeyed words, Dohga remained a knight. Ariel was greedy. She wasn't going to let North Emperor Dohga slip through her fingers. She told him off for creating a scene in the royal chambers and assigned him labor as punishment, but it was nothing very arduous.

It was thus that both Isolde and Dohga were able to put down roots. The Seven Knights of Asura became more tight-knit, which was a great success for Ariel. She owed favors to the royals she had solicited, but that was nothing. However, because of his marriage, Dohga's time for guarding the royal chambers plummeted. He went home on time every night, and when Isolde went away, he accompanied her without fail. As a result, Isolde ended up shifting into a role of something like Ariel's personal guard.

Isolde, however awkwardly, had agreed to marry Dohga. She imposed a dating period before they got married, so it was a year until the happy occasion took place. Because of the delay, even after they were married, rumors went around that it was all one-sided affection on Dohga's part, and Isolde didn't care for him much at all. Her attitude toward him in the palace stayed as chilly as ever. The rumors quickly fizzled out after an incident where Isolde accidentally called Dohga "darling" in front of the soldiers, before turning bright red and trying to correct herself. People speculated she warmed up when they were alone together.

And that is how Dohga and Isolde became husband and wife.

The Woman They Called the Mad Dog

Mushoku Tensei
redundant reincarnation

The Woman They Called the Mad Dog

I HEARD THAT MY FRIEND Dohga recently got married. North Emperor Dohga—the gentle strongman to whom I owed my life. To be honest, I was worried at first. An innocent guy like him? Some raven-hearted temptress must have tricked him. And if so, it'd be up to me to save him.

I decided to see what Ariel knew. I was all fired up to investigate this seducer of men when a letter arrived for Eris. It was from Isolde Cluel. Water Emperor Isolde—the wholesome beauty who'd assisted us in the battle in the Biheiril Kingdom. The letter mentioned her triumphant ascension to the title Water God and her inheritance of the name Reida. It also said that she had found love and gotten married...to Dohga.

Dohga, of all people, had made that willowy beauty his wife. Congratulations were in order. But even if she had helped us in the Biheiril Kingdom, who knew what nefarious things she was up to at night? You could never rule out that possibility.

I asked Eris what sort of woman she was. Eris told me she wasn't a bad person. This wasn't enough to reassure me, so I went to the Asura Kingdom to casually suss out Ariel's thoughts on the matter, made discreet inroads with Luke, and nonchalantly made inquiries with Ghislaine. I lurked in the shadows watching Dohga, went to introduce myself at the Water God training hall, and then put out feelers with the head of the Cluel family...

"My," Ariel said dryly, "don't you have a lot of free time?"

It wasn't like that! I wasn't doing this to kill time—I owed Dohga my life, and I wouldn't allow him to suffer!

Anyway, in the end, one fact emerged: Isolde was the sort to choose a man for his looks.

So you're a blackhearted temptress after all, Isolde... Don't think I'll take this lying down...

Only, the results of my investigations revealed that the two of them were totally in love.

Dohga seemed genuinely happy. Rumor had it, when there was no one around, Isolde called him "darling" and smothered him in kisses. Despite my intel that Isolde chose guys based on looks, she must have seen something in Dohga other than his face that made her choose him. She took a convoluted route to get him, but she'd finally found a soul mate.

In a similar vein, until Dohga saved my life, I'd thought he was a useless blockhead. *I'd* been blackhearted. *I'd* been the bad guy. How could I judge Isolde? Having arrived at that conclusion, I gave the couple my blessing and set off for home.

But wow, Isolde and Dohga...? You never knew who'd end up getting together. I mean, I never imagined I'd end up marrying three people. Misty-eyed about my own marriages, I made my way home.

Three days later:

"I wanna go to the beastfolk village!" That was Eris. News of Isolde's marriage had put her in cheerful spirits, and this was our habitual sofa lounging time.

"What's this, all of a sudden?" I asked, sitting up on Eris's right. On her left was Pursena, curled up and reading a book with her head resting on Eris's lap. Between the two of them, I didn't have quite enough room.

Linia and Pursena were both sort of like Eris's henchmen these days, but because Pursena was Leo's attendant, she was usually here and hanging on Eris like she was now.

Pursena was a bit like a dog, so she probably liked Eris's attention. However, Linia didn't like Eris. She was a bit like a cat, and Eris came on too strong. Right now, Leo was curled up at Eris's feet with Lucie and Sieg napping on top of him. Even at Eris's shouting, they showed no sign of stirring. Maybe they were used to it.

It was a positively domestic scene.

And yet. The beastfolk village? For Eris, that place was both a drug and a paradise. It'd go something like *We're at the beastfolk village! The beastfolk are very cute! Aw, look at the baby! Little baby! Can I have one?*

Dangerous stuff!

"Remember the last time we went, and I made friends with Linia's little sisters? I want to see how they're doing!"

Minitona and Tersena, wasn't it? That's right, the two of them had to have grown up into candidates for warrior chief by now, surpassing their older sisters. If Pursena hadn't lost her position, she might have been an advisor now rather than a candidate. She might even have been a high-powered career woman serving as warrior chief. A very different fate from lounging around on my couch.

She might have lost that position, but she was still second-in-command of my Ruquag's Mercenary Band. She worked herself to the bone in that role. The mercenary band's numbers had swelled, and it felt like Linia and Pursena's position had risen the more people they oversaw. They didn't seem all that anxious about their place in life.

"Remember? You said we'd go once Lara was bigger!"

"Well, I meant after she turned fifteen..."

"What's wrong with going sooner?"

"Well, I guess."

Lara was going to be their savior. To ensure that, she and Leo stayed so close, they practically read each other's minds. Maybe it wasn't a bad idea to foster close ties with the beastfolk from a young age.

But! "We can't just show up without warning," I pointed out.

"It'll be fine! Right, Pursena?"

"Just showing up in and of itself won't be a problem," she replied carelessly.

"No, you're coming too."

"I'll go, but that's not going to help."

"What, you don't mind?"

Last time, Pursena had gotten arrested for swiping from the village stores. There had been extenuating circumstances, so she was sentenced to be Leo's attendant. In theory, if she kept at it until Lara came of age, she'd be back in the running for leader of the tribe. It *did* seem like she'd fallen off the career ladder, though. It was hard to imagine the stubborn beastfolk would recognize Pursena as a leader if she just sauntered back in after years away.

"Boss, I'm second-in-command of Ruquag's Mercenary Band... You could even say I'm subleader of the pack. I don't love being lower in the pecking order than Linia, but I've gotta conduct myself with dignity around other packs."

"Wait, come on, you *are* in the running for leader of the Doldia Tribe..."

No way. She hadn't given up, had she? She wasn't thinking that, like, even if she couldn't be tribe leader, hey, second-in-command of the Ruquag Mercenaries was good enough, or something?

So far as the world's concerned, we're a minor enterprise, you know?

"Heh heh. Don't you see, Boss? I, the second-in-command of Ruquag's Mercenary Band, will become leader of the Doldia tribe. The Doldias will gain a connection with a powerful pack. This is how I will stand out from the rest when the leader's selected. My triumphant return, you might say!"

Given the Doldias were connected with me, they already had a connection to Ruquag's Mercenary Band...

But then again, how stable was that bond? It would probably be a weight off to have one of their own blood in both camps.

"Oh, but it might be better to wait a bit longer before taking the sacred beast and Miss Lara."

"Why's that?"

"For the beastfolk, the sacred beast setting out on a journey holds special significance. They'll want to make it grand, with a ceremony or a sort of festival. That day will be when they first behold the savior. It's significant."

So it wasn't a good idea to have Lara make her debut at this stage.

"The Doldia tribe will spend years getting ready for it. They'll ask all the tribes of the forest to help them to make a big thing of it."

"Right... I mean, I'm happy to contribute from a financial perspective."

My pocket money might not go far at a beastfolk festival, but I was the head of the Greyrat family. For the sake of my daughter's big day, I would bravely do what it took to secure the cash. That's right, I'd even beg my employer to let me borrow it.

"You can't. The Doldia tribe is proud. That's why they're the leaders of the beastfolk. They'll do it all themselves."

It was a custom or a convention or something then, huh? Well, if the Doldias were too proud to accept help, I wasn't about to get in their way.

"Still, you could at least go hammer out the arrangements now."

"True."

If I didn't know what sort of ceremony it would be, I wouldn't know how to get Lara to prepare for it. I didn't think it'd be dangerous, but I'd feel better knowing.

"Then I guess we'll pop over there."

"All right!"

Eris jumped to her feet, and Pursena went tumbling to the floor with a yowl. She must have crushed Leo's tail as she did so because Leo growled. Eris apologized profusely, and then Lara, bleary-eyed, raised her head and made grabby hands up at Daddy. I picked her up.

"Let's go!"

"Not so fast. We've got to get confirmation from Orsted first. He might be busy."

"Whaaat?!" Eris whined.

But I wasn't about to abandon my job to go enjoy myself. That said, it was unlikely the CEO would turn me down about anything regarding Lara. He'd never once told me, "If you've got time for that, you've got time for work." It was a bad idea to rely on that, though.

Eris was already at the door of the living room, but a thought suddenly struck her.

"Let's bring Ghislaine too!"

"She won't come, will she?"

I wasn't totally clear on what sort of treatment Ghislaine had received in the Doldia village, but given what I remembered of Gyes's attitude, there was bad blood there.

"Why not?" Eris demanded. "Ghislaine's an Asuran knight! She even had the gold armor last time! It'll be a triumphant return!"

"That's right," Pursena muttered. Without meeting anyone's eyes, she awkwardly fiddled with the tip of her tail. This was peer pressure. Her face said she absolutely knew how Ghislaine had been treated back in the village.

Ghislaine herself didn't come across as all that conflicted about the Doldia tribe. Gyes seemed to have reconsidered his opinion of her too, so it might be good for them to have the chance to have a nice moment together. At this rate, Ghislaine would go her whole life without returning to the village, then end up on her deathbed, whispering, "If only I'd gone home just once..."

"Okay. Let's ask her."

"Woo!" Eris strode triumphantly from the room. Leo followed her with Sieg still on his back. That left only

Pursena and Lara, who had fallen asleep again on my chest. So as not to wake my girl, I eased back down on the sofa. Pursena sat with us, like nothing had happened, and put her head on my lap. I shuffled my knees to get her off.

"Ow."

"You can't just put your head on the knees of a man's wife."

"Selfish! And you're the husband."

"I'm Eris's blushing bride, actually."

"Fuck off."

This isn't selfishness. What happens when you start to smell of pheromones in front of my baby girl, huh?

Pursena tilted her head to put her feet on my knees instead. *Eh, not so bad.* She wasn't in her wifely skirts today, so her legs were covered, and I liked the feel of Pursena's tail brushing against me.

"Just tell me one thing..." I said. "What do you guys think of Ghislaine?"

"I think my dad and the others have some hang-ups, but to us she's like a cool aunt. It's not everyday someone leaves the village to live by her sword and becomes a swordswoman. She's an inspiration to our generation."

"Huh. All right."

I wasn't totally comfortable about it, but if Pursena said so, I guess it made sense. Maybe I could manage some TLC. If Ghislaine said she didn't want to go, then that'd be that. I couldn't see her refusing if Eris invited her though, so I'd assume she was coming and go from there.

The CEO readily gave his approval. He even gave me a gift to take with me. The new hire wouldn't shut up—"Where are you going?! Who with?! Sword King Ghislaine! When's the fight?!" I figured even if I went into the details, he wouldn't get it, so I replied vaguely. It seemed to satisfy him. The kid was more of a chump than I'd thought.

The day arrived. Linia and Pursena came face-to-face with Ghislaine.

"It's an honor to meet you, mew! I'm Liniana Dedoldia, mew!"

"I've heard so much about you! I'm Pursena Adoldia!"

They were on their best behavior. It was like when a senior student came back for Sports Day after graduating.

"I've always admired how you left to make a name for yourself, mew!"

"We thought that one day, after we got ourselves known, we'd come and introduce ourselves!"

Ghislaine had the composure of a retired mob boss. She sure didn't play herself down, but she wasn't arrogant either—the stillness of a large guard dog. She was the same old Ghislaine I knew.

"Can you really go? It seemed like you had things to do..."

Ghislaine was at the parade grounds, deep in conversation with Sandor and Isolde about something. It had *looked* like she was busy...

"I'm teaching the knights new techniques."

"Oh, right. That was a thing, wasn't it?"

I'd heard about it from Ariel. Asura currently had three sword instructors: a Sword God Style practitioner, a Water God Style practitioner, and a North God Style practitioner. One of them was a geriatric man-child who had zero interest in teaching sword fighting and just wanted to order some kids around. With three warriors from three different styles, you could guess how they butted heads.

At Sandor's suggestion, they were trying something new: taking the best points of Sword God Style, Water God Style, and North God Style to develop a new sword fighting style for the knights of the Asura Kingdom. A Sword King, the current Water God, and the former

North God each taught their own styles, then the former North God would tie it all together. I thought they'd probably just end up with a new North God sect, but Ghislaine said, "I've taught you the way I know how to do it. I'm leaving the details to him." Ghislaine's presence was an unexpectedly good influence. She took her job seriously, but she wasn't delicate about it. The Asuran knights' sword fighting style had wound up mainly modeled on Sword God Style with some Water God Style and North God Style worked in.

"Aren't you busy enough with that?"

"Oh, absolutely. I just can't say no to little Eris," Ghislaine said. I followed her gaze and sure enough, there she was, arms folded and in a mood.

"I'm not a little miss anymore!"

"True, you're married now," Ghislaine said with a laugh. Linia and Pursena snickered.

"What?" Eris demanded.

"You seem purr-leased today, mew!"

"You're such a kid."

"Whatever..." Without changing her pose, Eris turned her head, pouting. Eris still adored Ghislaine. She had a new home now and a family, but to Eris, Ghislaine was the only family she had left from the Citadel of Roa in

Fittoa, her childhood home. Ghislaine was like a fond extended relative. The thought of getting to go on another journey with her thrilled Eris.

"Shall we get going, then?" I said. And so, we set out once more for the Doldia village in the Great Forest.

Ghislaine

I DEFINITELY DIDN'T HAVE what you'll call a smooth start to life.

Every now and then, the beastfolk give birth to children known as "beastlings." There's no cosmic reason behind them. They are born with fangs and lash out like aggressive, terrified animals. They never learn to speak.

I was one of them. I hardly have any memories of my childhood, but in my earliest memories, my heart was dominated by rage. Everything about my body was constricting and torturous. I turned that anger on everyone around me—they were all my enemy. I never thought about why it felt that way. I still don't know now. To this day, that anger still lurks in the depths of my heart, rearing its ugly head at every irritation. All I remember is the angry yelling of adults and the fear on the faces of my brothers.

Most beastlings settle down as they grow up. By the time they turn five or so, their only symptoms are being a bit slow and bad-tempered. Not me. My fifth birthday came and went, and I was still running wild. I was a terror. Five is an age where you're more or less able to use a little reason, but I didn't have a thought in my head. I was constantly flying into tantrums and nearly killed the other kids.

There was no reason for it; if I didn't like someone's face, I just acted. In Doldia Village, unruly children like me are stripped naked and doused with icy water. Sometimes, they're even shut up all night in a dark barn. That usually settles us down—maybe it's instinctual. But beastlings are different, or at least I was. I don't know. I guess some others may have broken under that kind of treatment.

Kids like me are so difficult, sometimes they meet with "accidents." They're left out in the forest at night when it's crawling with monsters. Things like that.

They tried to do it to me too… No, they *did* do it to me. I didn't understand what was happening, but I somehow knew that the whole village was trying to drive me away—I do have a survival instinct, after all. But I didn't die, thanks to a traveling swordsman in the middle of his warrior's training—I was taken in by Gall Falion.

"You don't want her? Then give her to me," he said. He adopted me like I was a rejected stray and took me from the village. Don't think I took to him just because he rescued me. I wouldn't have been a cute kid. I bit and scratched and howled, but Gall Falion brushed that off, subdued me, put a collar around my neck, and put a sword in my hands.

Then, he said, "If you ask me, you're made to swing a sword. You get in a fight, you use this."

Looking back, Gall Falion—my master—must have been crazy. Just think—he gave me a sword, then told me I could use it on whatever I wanted. This is *me* we're talking about. I wouldn't have trusted me with one.

Still, he wasn't completely reckless with others' lives. For a while, we steered clear of inhabited areas. We roamed about the forest hunting beasts and monsters.

In the morning, my master beat me to a pulp. When that was over, he dragged me in front of some monster and made me fight it, and I fought for my life. Sometimes I got injured, but I was never badly hurt, and I didn't die. He must have had a sense of how strong I was in relation to the monsters we fought, because he only ever pitted me against monsters I could beat by the skin of my teeth.

In the afternoon, we ate the monsters we'd killed. After that, I could do as I pleased for the rest of the day.

At the start, I attacked my master and tried to kill him. I couldn't have been more outmatched. He shrugged me off, then knocked me around a bit. But even that wasn't enough to cow me. I got up and went at him again. As a rule, he met my attacks with a grin on his face. He never gave me any formal instruction in how to use my sword, and I wouldn't have listened anyway. There was one case that was different, though: when I attacked him without my sword. If I tossed aside my sword during a fight, he'd click his tongue once, then throw an even harder punch than usual and knock me out cold. When I woke up, my sword would be lashed to my hand.

I was an idiot, but after a year of that, even I learned a little. I knew I couldn't beat him, and if I lashed out randomly, I'd only get a thrashing. It's incredible I could reason that much, but I guess even a beast knows when it's beat.

That was my very first lesson in life. Around that time, my sword instruction began. He used words: "Do this, do that. Think rationally. Wear your opponent down steadily, one move at a time..."

I'm not clever. For every hundred lessons, I remembered ten. That's hardly changed, if I'm being honest.

But my master was patient. He must have known that even I would get better if we drilled the same thing over and over again. I suppose I had talent, because I improved rapidly. At the same time, perhaps thanks to the training, I began, little by little, to see the beastling influence fade.

Maybe it was working off my impulses every day running around killing monsters because, when I saw other people, I didn't get as enraged as I had. Or, well, that only happened if they didn't try to speak to me—if they did, *then* I'd attack. Eventually, my master decided that I was safe to take into town. I was more used to people, but it was suffocating at first. More often than not, I was met with hostility. I still feel that way.

My master told me, "Ignore 'em. Being strong'll shut 'em up. They'll trip over themselves to kiss your ass. Some'll even come attach themselves to you like puppies."

The idea of a stranger attaching to me like a puppy was disgusting.

Then I met Eris.

I was wrong. It's better to be loved than hated.

Anyway, I was finally able to enter the fringes of society, although I still hadn't had a real conversation with anyone. I didn't have a lot of words at my disposal. Okay, to qualify, my master always talked to me in the beastfolk tongue, and I'd lived in the Doldia village until I was ten, so I did know the language. I'd just never talked *with* anyone. I don't remember when I had my first real conversation, but it was probably with my master. I might have been swearing at him or asking a question—I don't recall. But this was my master. He'd have answered without making a big deal out of the event, which is why it didn't register for me.

Around when I learned how to talk to people, our journey came to an end. We arrived at the Sword Sanctum, and that's where I made my new home. There was no need for conversation, and I could knock out anyone who screwed with me. In the Doldia village, people had given me nasty looks for that, but here, it got me respect. No one complained, and I could do what I wanted. If I just kept knocking people out, the Sword Sanctum was paradise. Simple enough.

But then, maybe because I'd gotten too comfortable, my master turned me out on my ear. It was the law of the Sword Sanctum that once you got above Sword Saint, you went out to complete your warrior's training, so that might be what it was. No one told me anything about that. I was just thrown out. Told to go see the outside world. I went out into the world, became an adventurer, met Paul. Then we parted ways.

"And then you met me!" said Eris cheerfully.

In a carriage, rolling along the road to the Sword Sanctum through the Great Forest, I shared my life story. I had to wonder if it was really interesting or not, but Eris was listening, rapt. Linia and Pursena were listening with interest too.

"That's right," I said. Eris looked smug that she knew the rest of the tale. When I'd gotten to the part about visiting the Sword Sanctum, she'd said knowingly, "Yeah! When you beat 'em down enough times, they respect you!"

The Sword Sanctum was like a second home both for me and for Eris. Scratch that, for Eris it was a *third* home. For me... It was my first.

Linia and Pursena's eyes were glazing over a bit, their mouths half open. A long time ago, it would have filled me with rage. Now, I didn't mind so much.

"Mewww, what a heroic life! If it were me, I'd have turned into a good girl the moment they threw water on me, mew. Now that I remember, I totally did, mew."

"All they had to do with me was send me to bed without dinner. But unlike Linia, I was always a good girl, so I was just doing what came naturally."

"I'm a good girl too, mew."

"You're both good girls compared to me," I said. They both bashfully scratched the backs of their heads.

"After that, I met Rudeus. And just as I finally had my feet under me, the Displacement Incident happened."

"That's right! You reunited with Eris in Fittoa, then went back to the Sword Sanctum to train, mew?"

"Yeah, that's right."

"When you finished your training, you and the boss went to Asura and you became Ariel's servant, right?"

"More or less. When everything was over, Her Majesty told me she wanted me to stay and gave me this armor."

I was now clad in golden armor. When I told Queen Ariel I was going to the Doldia village, she brought it out, saying I absolutely had to wear it. I'd taken it off to travel, but now that we were almost there, I'd put it back on.

"Ariel's clever, mew."

"Yeah. It's important to show off your strength."

Linia and Pursena were young Doldians. Oh, right—Linia was Gyes's daughter. They'd each gone to school and graduated top of their class. Now, they managed the mercenary band and had over five hundred people working under them. The mercenary band worked for Rudeus, so that basically meant they worked for Orsted. They were clever girls who had been given responsibility for a pack by a Great Power. They were resounding successes. Gyes must've been proud. I wished I remembered his face.

"No one would believe the Ghislaine they knew rose to become one of the Seven Knights of Asura, mew."

"Yeah. But one look at that sparkly gold armor really drives it home. You've even got the Asuran crest on there. This is your triumphant return. Everyone's gonna see you differently."

"Oh...?" I didn't really get it, but if these two talented Doldians said so, it had to be true.

"Yeah! I won't let anyone say different!" Eris's breathing had been heavier ever since I put this armor on. She said it suited me, but it was too shiny for me... I supposed it'd come handy in the dark.

Still, if I said I wasn't nervous, I'd be lying. The Doldia Village I remembered had rejected me.

"Hrm?"

"Oh."

"We're close," Linia said. We still couldn't see anything, but there was a familiar smell in the air: the smell of Doldia Village. Bad memories. The base of my tail began to itch, and I felt a growl rise to the back of my throat. The urge to run gripped me.

"What do you think, Rudeus?" I asked. "Will it be okay?"

That wasn't a question the old me would have asked. Maybe I'd asked Paul something like that way back when I was part of Fangs of the Black Wolf. How had he answered, again?

"Eh?" Rudeus answered from where he sat in the driver's box. "Oh, yeah, it should be? If it starts looking dicey, I'll sort it out. Leave it to me."

Now I remembered. Paul had usually replied that way too. *Eh, it'll be fine. Even if it's not, things will work out somehow.*

It felt like just yesterday that Geese, Talhand, and Elinalise had rolled their eyes and sighed at him, but in the end, he'd been right. The only time it hadn't worked out was when Paul married Zenith, then died.

"Yeah, it should be fine... I've got the present from Sir Orsted for them and a box of sweets... Oh! Hmm, we've got Linia and Pursena with us too..." The words filtered through from the driver's box.

Rudeus seemed a bit out of sorts. He was holding his stomach. It was a tic he had when I told him stories from my past. Who knew what that was about?

He'd really grown up well. He'd been a clever kid who'd grown up clever, and he had a knack for getting on in the world. Now, he was one of the Seven Great Powers and Orsted's right-hand man. If he said he'd sort it out, that's what he'd do.

"So even *you* get nervous sometimes, Ghislaine, mew."

"I get it. Dad and the others are stuck in their ways. They find it really hard to accept Doldias like us who've gotten used to city life, I think."

"Don't worry, Rudeus is amazing!" Eris said, sounding so much like I remembered her that it drew a smile out of me. Looking out the window, I could see a number of warriors running alongside the carriage. I could tell they were watching us, hiding in the shadows of the trees, lithe as cats and ferocious as tigers. They were downwind. I couldn't smell them, but the scent that hung over this whole area was unmistakably that of one tribe—I had come home to Doldia Village.

Gyes

FOR DOLDIAS OF MY GENERATION, Ghislaine Dedoldia was an object of fear and scorn. She was abnormal beyond anything we'd ever seen. Children like her were traditionally called "beastlings," but her? She was something else entirely—not even a person.

It wasn't just that words didn't get through to her. Nothing we did to communicate with her worked, and we couldn't tell what she wanted. She always smelled of anger and frustration, and if you so much as met her eyes, she'd attack. She nearly killed me countless times.

Every time she attempted it, she was stripped naked and doused in city water, then shut up in a barn, but nothing helped. That punishment was a surefire extinguisher of rage, and it calmed people down so quickly, you felt sorry for them. It worked on *everyone*.

But not her.

You could drench her in water or shut her up in the dark all day, but she only grew more furious, her rampages more intense. Nothing changed when our father made the decision to kill her, only to fail in the attempt. When she was taken away by an odd traveling swordsman, I felt overwhelming relief. She hadn't died in Doldia Village, but I could rest easy. A creature like that wouldn't live long, I thought. She'd die in some lonely ditch.

So when the name of "Sword King Ghislaine" came to us on the wind, I didn't think anything of it. Ghislaine, swordswoman of the Doldia tribe? It wasn't possible.

I figured some idiot who knew Ghislaine's name had stolen it to gild their reputation.

With a mix of fear and horror, our generation stayed in denial. When the children heard the stories of Ghislaine, their eyes lit up. They didn't know her, so to them, it must have sounded like someone who had left the village and made her fortune. In any case, I'd never imagined she'd make it to adulthood. There was no way a creature who left that much destruction in its wake would survive. Now that I was grown, I understood how pitiful she had been as a beastling, but still, the resentment was still lodged tightly in the depths of my heart. Every time I heard her name, I thought, *Ghislaine, finding success out in the world? Like hell.*

More than ten years ago, human children had brought a demon warrior to us. That was how I'd heard the story of Ghislaine's unbelievable life. *Ghislaine,* teaching children how to fight with swords while she, in turn, learned how to read and do sums... *Is this a joke?* I thought. *She'd eat children as soon as look at them. It's in her nature.*

But one of the children—Rudeus Greyrat—told me something. He said, "People can change."

Impossible. I knew it had to be someone who had assumed the name. Or rather, I'd hoped as much.

Now, Ghislaine was in front of me.

With her were Master Rudeus and Miss Eris. My silly daughters had even come along too. When I asked why they had come, they said it was to discuss what would happen when Lara, Rudeus's daughter and the sacred beast's chosen savior, came of age.

It was true that the Doldia tribe held a ceremony upon the birth of the savior, the sacred beast's companion. The whole of the Great Forest would be swept up in the affair. It was a great undertaking requiring several years of preparation. Master Rudeus was another species, and I doubted he had especially profound knowledge of the Doldia tribe, but he offered his assistance. It was much appreciated. I supposed Linia and Pursena had brought him around.

After they left the village to attend to the sacred beast, I had heard nothing of them, but they seemed to have done well for themselves. While they were there, they were even serving Master Rudeus as leaders of a pack called Ruquag's Mercenary Band. As a parent, I was proud. It wouldn't be enough to erase their mistakes from last time, but it was an achievement great enough to satisfy Minitona and Tersena, whose tensions over choosing the next chief were mounting. Minitona and Tersena were ambitious. They'd train even harder after seeing the girls' success.

"When the savior... When *Lara* sets off on her journey with the Sacred Beast, all the tribes living in the Great Forest must consent to and be present at the ceremony. With all your connections, Master Rudeus, we would be most grateful for your assistance."

"I'm glad to hear it. I thought you might tell me you would do it all yourselves and I'd have to shut up and hand her over."

"Ha ha. I might have said as much to another human, but not to one who understands how much this ceremony means to the Doldia tribe."

My talk with Rudeus was pleasant. Perhaps it was my imagination, but it seemed as though he was delicately avoiding the subject of Ghislaine. It smelled of that sort of thing.

"All right, I'll notify all the tribes and you'll handle the preparations. Is Lara's outfit the only thing we need to get ready, then?"

"There is no need; there is traditional garb. Only..."

"What is it?"

"The monsters we use for the material live in the depths of the Great Forest. For generations, it has been the warrior chief who goes to hunt them. Now, well, the village has no warrior chief..."

"Ah..."

I shot a glance at my daughters. One looked the other way, as if she hadn't heard. The other was sucking on a meaty bone she'd brought herself. Good-for-nothings.

"I have not yet determined the details, but in a few years' time, I wish to send out a hunt for these monsters that will also serve as the selection ritual for the warrior chief."

"That will be quite the headache."

"You understand me, then?"

Master Rudeus gave a deep nod. I'd thought this the last time we met, but he'd grown. It was impossible to believe he was the same boy who had hidden in a wooden chest to spy on my daughters as they bathed. What a disgrace my daughters were by comparison. When I anticipated we'd have more dealings with the humans, I sent them to a far-off school so that they might also learn about society. This is how they'd squandered that education. But while they looked like good-for-nothings to me, in human society, they were the leader and second-in-command of a mercenary band—pack leaders. Perhaps I was the problem.

"You don't mind doing it like that, Pursena?"

"Fine with me. I mean, I'd be happy to do it now. I'll wipe the floor with Minitona and Tersena."

"You seem confident."

"Why wouldn't I be? Who do you think I train with?" She looked at Miss Eris... Had she looked at Ghislaine? Could it be that Ghislaine hadn't just trained Eris, but Pursena as well...?

"I haven't been in the Great Forest for a while, so it might take me a while to find the monsters. That won't be too hard to get over."

Beside Pursena, Linia nodded with a knowing smirk. In the past, when Pursena got like this, Linia would have immediately teased her or insisted that she was better. Now she just nodded quietly. They were that serious, then. I had my misgivings, but if they were preparing properly, I was pleased.

So there was a chance that Pursena would become warrior chief. I wasn't sure how to feel about that.

"Then when the day is set, I will send word."

"Gotcha. I'll leave a magician from the mercenary band here as a liaison."

Master Rudeus intended to leave a magical message tablet in the village, and I was meant to keep in touch that way. How very convenient that Linia and Pursena were in a position to make use of such things. The two of them had been away from Doldia Village for a long time, so their habits of thinking weren't very natural to me, but new knowledge and goods could breathe new life into the village. That could not be a bad thing.

The conversation stalled. We had discussed the ceremony and the selection of the warrior chief. There was nothing left. I wanted to tell them to go have a meal and rest here for the night, but...

Ghislaine's silent presence through all of this unsettled me. The Ghislaine I knew could never have sat quietly for such a long time—she would have gone wild halfway through. Someone would have gotten hurt. I wanted to question if this was really her, but there was no doubting her distinctive scent. It made the base of my tail itch. Long ago, I would have run away as soon as I caught a whiff of it approaching...

"Ghislaine." Her name came to my lips unbidden. We would get nowhere sitting here in silence. I was the chief of the Doldia tribe now. My silence would have shamed me.

"What?" Ghislaine's tail twitched, and she looked at me.

"How dare you show your face?"

A cold sweat broke out on my back as I spoke. The Ghislaine of old would have beat me half to death just for that. Clearly, she'd spent these years honing herself like a blade. If this were our first meeting, I would have thought she was someone I ought to respect. But if the Ghislaine from long ago wielded this strength, she would have used it to take my head. She might have murdered any one of the villagers. I ought to cast her out before she did any damage.

But Miss Eris had gone out of her way to bring Ghislaine here. I had to face her—as both someone who refused to forget what she was, and as the current chief.

Eris began to rise, her hand on her sword, but she thought better of it. She sat back down, her brow furrowed. Ghislaine had thrown her hand out to hold her back.

At length, Ghislaine spoke. "I trained at the Sword Sanctum and earned the title of Sword King. My strength is recognized. Now I serve the ruler of the Asura Kingdom. Look at my armor. It is a very good post. They treat me well... That is how I dare." She spoke a little haltingly, but her face was impassive.

"I thought you'd bear a grudge against this village..."

"A grudge? Why?" Ghislaine cocked her head at me.

"*Why?* We drove you out. We tried to kill you. Remember?"

Ghislaine paused, then said, "What else would you do with a beast who couldn't understand language? I can't begrudge you that." She went on matter-of-factly, "When I was granted the title of Sword King, my master told me something. He said, 'You are Sword King Ghislaine of the Doldia tribe. Use that name with pride. Whenever you swear an oath, you swear it on the Doldias.'"

"*Pride?*"

"Yeah."

Go to hell. You don't get to call yourself a Doldia, I wanted to shout, but I couldn't. Why? I didn't know. Ghislaine's words had been strangely comforting.

"The name of the Doldia tribe has helped me and never hindered me. I bear no grudge."

A memory of my youth, back before I became warrior chief, came back to me, way back when the rumors of Sword King Ghislaine had wafted into the village. The name had a degree of notoriety attached to it, but the stories were not shameful. On the contrary, most of them were glowing. One told of how she had conquered a challenging labyrinth. As an adventurer, that was a great honor. Ghislaine *of the Doldia tribe* had done it.

Like hell that could be true. It must be an imposter. I'd said it then, and the others of my generation had joined their voices with mine. But had I not felt just the slightest bit of pride? I was proud to be part of the Doldia tribe. Had I not been pleased to hear that one of our own was making a name for herself? Even if she had been cast out...

"If anything, I feel ashamed. I'm sorry I'm such a fool." Ghislaine bowed her head.

She apologized. *Ghislaine* had apologized.

"I... I see." I shut my eyes.

It was I who had been a fool. Ghislaine had only been suffering from the worst symptoms of being a beastling. Even our parents gave her up as a hopeless case, but beastlings take time. Now that she'd had it, Ghislaine had grown up into a fine woman. The village cast her out, but she'd gotten her sense and grew. Not only that, but she was proud to be a Doldia. She still announced her heritage now that she'd acquired fame. She held her head high. Today, on this day, she had come home.

This was a good faith effort. I knew what to say to her.

"Sword King Ghislaine Dedoldia. I am glad to see you back in the Doldia village, and as its chief, Gyes Dedoldia, I welcome you."

"You're too kind." Ghislaine stood up, then dropped to one knee and bowed her head. That was how the swordsmen of the Sword God Style greeted a person of higher rank. It was proper and a great honor for me—and from *Ghislaine.*

Ghislaine saw me as her superior...?

"Stay here tonight, and then on the morrow, tell me of your travels."

"As you wish. I have many interesting tales."

I welcomed her. I could not forget all that had happened between us, but it was time to step aside for the next generation. I couldn't help but worry about my daughters, who were of that generation... But if Ghislaine could change, maybe they could as well. After all, my father and my grandfather before him would have had worries like mine, but they served their time as chief. My time had come, and theirs would, too...

That was how the homecoming of Ghislaine Dedoldia came to pass.

Mushoku
Tensei
redundant
reincarnation

ABOUT THE AUTHOR

Rifujin na Magonote

Resides in Gifu Prefecture. Loves fighting games and cream puffs. Inspired by other published works on the website *Let's Be Novelists*, they created the webnovel *Mushoku Tensei*. In 2022, the 26th and final volume of the main series was released, and from 2023, they began *Mushoku Tensei: Redundant Reincarnation*, a collection of stories set after the main series.

"Nope! Not over yet!" said the author.